Bestselling author Melanie Ann was born in Richmond, Virginia but now calls Florida and Greece home. Melanie has done extensive research into the early Christian, late antiquity and medieval periods of history and has published numerous articles and books on the subjects. One of her favorite things to do is to visit old libraries around the world—New York, London, Athens, Washington D.C.—in order to see primary sources of information. She also loves exploring castles, ancient church buildings and writing about the people who lived and worked in times past. Her eclectic array of books—inspirational romances, children's books, nonfiction, etc.—reflect this.

Books by Melanie Ann Include:

FROM GREECE WITH LOVE Inspirational romance series
1) The Village Doctor
2) New York Welcome (Coming September, 2022)
3) Love Comes Unexpectedly (Coming September, 2022)

SAVING MAIN STREET: The Store Next Door (modern inspirational romance)
SAINT NICHOLAS & CHRISTMAS: The Teenager Who Gave Us the Celebration (biography)
THE SKELETON KEY KEEPERS: Clues to the Chalice (children's detective novel)
DOUBLECLICK TWINS: Journey to Bethlehem (children's Christian time-travel novel)

From Greece with Love

The Village Doctor

Christian Romance
with
Mood Boards

Set in a Mountain Village in Greece during the Summertime

"Enjoy a trip to Greece from the comfort of your own home!"

Melanie Ann

"And we know that all things work together for good to those who love God, to those who are the called according to *His* purpose..." **Romans 8:28 (NKJV)**

A note from the author;

I'd love to hear from you. If you enjoyed reading this book please leave an Amazon Review telling me how this story might have touched your life or made your day better.

ISBN: 9798837840289
THE VILLAGE DOCTOR

Unless otherwise stated, Scripture is taken from the Authorized Version of the King James Bible. Disclaimer: Any and all errors are purely unintentional. This is a work of pure fiction. The characters and events portrayed in this book are fictitious. Any similarity to real persons, living or dead, is coincidental and not intended by the author.

Mood Boards: Designed using CanvaPro / Cover Photo: CanvaPro; Brian Raggatt from Getty Images / Edited by: Jane Lott
Printed in the United States of America

PREFACE

Although a work of fiction, this story is based on my time in a Greek mountain village while my husband completed his compulsory "rural physician service." This was the country's way of ensuring that medical care was made available to people even in remote locations. We had our pick of some fabulous locations—in resort areas, islands, etc—but coming from America and wanting to "time travel" back in time, the idea of living in a remote mountain village, one that hadn't changed much in centuries out in the wilds of the high mountains of Greece, really appealed to me. It was a decision we never regretted for it was a way of life that was disappearing, not just in Greece, but in the entire western world. It was an extremely special time, a time when minimalism and sustainability weren't words people used, but rather the way of normal everyday life.

As such, "The Village Doctor" is a retro love story set in the 1990s. Taking place on the eve of the "digital revolution" it is our world before the internet was widely used and a smartphone was in most everyone's hand. A sweeter world? Maybe. But as is the way with looking back in time, our eyes are often covered with rose-tinted glasses.

However, it would be truthful to say that Greece *was* a very sweet place during the 1990s. It was a good period in the country's very long history, a time when general crime was practically zero, when people both in the countryside and cities could sleep with their windows open on hot summer nights or even out on their verandas, and a time when there was nowhere unsafe to walk in the entire country of cities, mountains, coasts and islands…unless as in this story, you landed yourself in the middle of a rural mountain village's feud! Such feuds were about the only crimes in Greece at that time, and they were, as shown in this book, a law unto themselves and had to be worked out within the warring clans of the villages.

Someday, I promise to write my autobiography about the time I spent as the wife of the rural doctor in a Greek mountain village. But until then, I am grateful to share with you, "The Village Doctor," which accurately portrays the emotions and life of a rural mountain village in Greece during the last years of the last century. I hope this story in some way touches your heart, adds to you day and makes you smile.

Note:
Each chapter opens with a "mood board" made up of photos. They are not intended to be exact representations of characters or places, but rather are to evoke the feeling and setting of the chapters. See the key at the end of the book for references. Do you agree with my choices? Please let me know at MelanieAnnAuthor@gmail.com and join my mailing list to get updates about future stories in the *From Greece with Love* series (and other books) and enter the drawing (to be held July 1, 2023) for an 8" reproduction of an ancient Greek amphora similar to the following.

Contents

Chapter 1—Simple Life

Early 1990s

The wide mountain valley shimmered and glowed in the heat of the summer day like wishes from her many dreams.

Beautiful, picture perfect, pastel and soft, timeless, and yet ever changing, it was also somehow familiar to Allie, even though she knew she had never visited it before. Her fingers smoothed down a section of peeling leather on the old bus' seat while she let her eyes, now narrowed against the strong glare of the sun, scan the landscape before her.

Ramrod cypress trees stood guard over ceramic-roofed peasants' sheds, while graceful groves of silver-clothed olive trees sat like a chorus of waiting ballerinas in the stillness of the day. Church-topped hills with whitewashed villages gleaming below in the strong summer sun—crinolines on a Victorian lady—dotted the landscape all the way to where tall, tranquil mountains formed a demarcation line with the rest of the world.

It was a world unto itself, a land of enchantment, of wonder. Allie's lips formed an amazed *O* as she realized that it didn't remind her of an actual place but rather of illustrations in her much-treasured volume, *Collection of Classic Fairy Tales*. The book had belonged to her mother and was even now making this remarkable journey with Allie in the luggage compartment of the ancient bus.

She settled deeper into the worn seat as a smile, a slow smile of satisfaction, of anticipation, lifted the corners of her lips. Allie Alexander, M.D., recognized that, for her, the Grecian countryside was the most enchanting place on earth. It was the

Shangri-La she had been searching for, wanting, for as long as she could remember. At that moment she knew she had made the correct decision—was indeed following the path God had laid out for her—in becoming a country doctor here.

Born and raised in New York City, Allie had left America for the home of her father's birth to attend medical school and residency in Athens. But after having been falsely accused of ethical misconduct by a patient—a soccer star—Allie knew the time had come for her to seek the simpler, more basic lifestyle for which she had always yearned.

To hear the singing of the birds in the morning rather than the grinding and groaning of the trash collector's truck, to live where something new awaited her at every curve in the road, to work where her knowledge of medicine made a difference to individuals whose faces and names she knew—not just to unknown people who matched impersonal numbers on a form—was a way of living Allie had desired for as long as she could remember. Like one knowing she was moving in God's will, she clasped her hands together and thought how she had finally found it.

She had signed a year-long contract to become a member of Greece's Rural Physician Service. She was now on her way to her new home, Kastro, a remote village located high in the mystic mountains above her. With the clear, dry air softly bathing her face and with her nose savoring the complimentary fragrances of the heated earth and its trees—a delicate mix of rock and pine that reminded her of a man's expensive aftershave—Allie thought she just might like to stay forever.

The bus rounded a bend, and Allie spied a medieval castle atop a distant mountain. Excited, she sat up in her seat. She loved castles, and this one didn't disappoint. It seemed to float ethereally in the sky, as if it had been built on something other than the mountain beneath it. With turrets and parapets sharply defined, it was the artist's finishing touch on the actual canvas before her, and whimsically Allie thought the only thing missing from this land of delicate beauty and unparalleled charm was a prince on a white horse.

Allie wouldn't mind her very own prince…

As long as he wasn't a patient of hers.

She would guard herself and her professionalism just as soundly as the walls of the fortress that loomed above had once protected the land surrounding it.

The bus rolled to a stop, but looking around, Allie couldn't understand why. A steep cliff fell to her left, while a dense forest was to her right. As far as she could tell, they were in the middle of nowhere, without even a sign to mark the spot as a bus stop.

But the only other passenger aboard, a man clutching two hens and wearing an old felt hat that had seen better days, recognized this no-man's-land as his own. He was disembarking, something the squiggling, squawking chickens were making difficult. With tough salt-and-pepper whiskers dotting his face and with skin leathery from spending much of his life outdoors, he more resembled a backwoodsman than a chicken farmer.

Cluck, cluck, cluck! The birds screamed with crescendo force, and the hitherto quiet man shouted back at them in a manner Allie thought similar to his fowl friends. Their wings flapped and their bodies twisted and turned in ways Allie wouldn't have believed possible if she hadn't been an eyewitness. She was reminded of the visiting Chinese acrobats her father had taken her to see at Madison Square Garden when she was a child. Those performers had been dressed up as chickens. Watching these real birds, Allie finally understood where their crazy choreography had come from.

But there hadn't been feathers floating around at that long-ago show as there were at this one. Soft and fluffy bits glided all around the bus like large snowflakes. The scene was different from anything Allie had experienced—something that might come from Lewis Carroll's crazy Wonderland. A cloud of downy fluff landed on Allie's wrist, tickling her sensitive skin. She could feel laughter ready to escape her.

But since the backwoodsman did not look like a man who would appreciate someone finding humor in the situation, Allie swallowed hard. She waved wayward feathers away from her nose and pointed her face in the direction of the staid safety of the castle, leaving the woodsman to a private, if inglorious, exit.

Her vision didn't reach the mighty bulwark on the summit, though.

It was blocked by the imposing form of a man outside her window.

A man who sat upon a horse.

Allie blinked.

A white horse.

Her gaze didn't spend more than half a moment on the beast. It went back to the man. And she was certain, absolutely sure, that Cinderella's prince could not have looked any better. With hair as dark as midnight and eyes that held the light of the stars in them, he was a perfect specimen of mankind.

When his lips curved into a smile, something inside of Allie jumped in response. She smiled back, and that age-old communication signaling a want, a desire to know someone better, passed between them like a fusion. His dark eyes reached out to hers, touched hers. Little shivers of pleasure ran up Allie's bare arms and down her spine, making her feel more womanly than she had felt in a very long time. She liked the sensation. She welcomed it.

That there was quick chemistry between them was evident to her scientific mind, although it didn't require her knowledge of science to figure that out. Science had nothing to do with what she was feeling. It was something basic, an impulse between a man and a woman, a feeling that probably went all the way back to Adam and Eve.

As the old bus ground into gear and slowly continued its journey up the mountain, their gaze remained connected until a turn in the road severed it.

Sighing, Allie sank back into the hot leather seat. She thoughtfully ran her right hand down the lengths of her double French braids as she wondered about him, who he was, what he believed. Slowly, her lips curved upward.

If her father had seen it, he would have looked at her with his love-filled eyes and told her that she was wearing her mysterious Mona Lisa smile. Actually, he would have told her that the one Leonardo da Vinci had painted on his portrait of the woman named Mona Lisa had nothing on the actual smile that decorated her face.

It was a smile created by Allie's decision: For Allie knew then and there that she liked country life.

She glanced over her shoulder in the direction of the prince. She liked it a lot.

***

"Einai koukla—she's a doll." Petros spoke to his friend Stavros and nodded after the belching bus while struggling to keep his

chickens from escaping his grip. Perspiration dripped from beneath his old felt hat and down his chin, but he ignored it.

Stavros glanced away from the noisy vehicle to the woodsman. He'd enjoyed flirting with the beautiful stranger through the window, but he hadn't wanted anyone witnessing it. Although he knew that if anyone had to see him making a fool of himself over some unknown woman, Petros was the one to do so. Petros was a recluse, a man who minded his own business. He'd never spread rumors. Suspecting that the very personality trait he admired in the other man would most likely render his question unanswered, Stavros asked anyway. "Do you know who she is?" He clicked his tongue to control his prancing horse. Charger didn't like being idle.

Petros shrugged his bony shoulders, showing that it was no concern of his. "Most likely somebody's relative who has come from the city to make fun of us country yokels," he replied as expected and started walking toward a woodland path that was barely visible from the road, one squabbling hen now securely placed under each arm.

Stavros regarded his friend's straight back thoughtfully. Petros had a pride that was as hard as the oak forest in which he lived. Unfortunately, he had an anger that was equally rigid. When no one in the village had been able to save his wife and newborn baby on a snowbound winter day three years earlier, he'd packed up his brood of four children and moved up onto the mountain.

Stavros understood his motives. He'd done something similar himself at around the same time by leaving Georgetown outside of Washington, D.C., and moving to his father's ancestral home in Greece. But it was a move that had been positive for his family, and thanks to his computer and satellite hookup, he wasn't cut off from the rest of the world. He corresponded by e-mail with his mother and numerous friends and business associates in the United States practically every day.

Contrarily, Stavros wasn't so sure it was good for Petros's family to be up on the mountain totally packed away from civilization. His house—an old, stone structure from the nineteenth century—didn't even have electricity.

A chicken suddenly lunged out its neck and pecked Petros on his nose, almost making good her escape. "You scrawny creature!" Petros shouted, catching the loudly complaining hen by her thin legs. "I'll make you into soup!"

Stavros chuckled, a sound barely heard above the din. "Are you starting a chicken farm?"

Petros swung around, disgust making his weathered nose flare. "You know I'm not. Maria wants them for eggs," he snapped out, referring to his sixteen-year-old daughter.

Stavros frowned. Maria was Petros's oldest, and since Petros's wife had died, Stavros knew that she had been looking after her younger brothers and sister. "When are you going to move those children back to the village?"

"When I have a good enough reason to move them, I will," Petros shot out.

Frown lines cut across Stavros's face. "They need to be in school," he pressed.

"Maria teaches them."

"But who teaches Maria?" Stavros returned.

Petros swung away from Stavros. "Mind your own mind," he mumbled, just before disappearing into the dense pine forest. The trees closed in upon him within seconds, leaving no indication a man had just walked through.

Stavros blew out air through his teeth. He knew to "mind his own mind" was good advice—advice he himself often handed out.

He leaned forward and absently rubbed Charger's neck. He and Petros were a lot alike. He frowned and sat up straight. He wasn't so sure if that was a good thing.

The flash of the sun on the rusty chrome of the bus drew his attention up the mountain to where the moving metal contraption came into view on yet another curve as it snaked its way up the range. Squinting up at it, Stavros admitted how the woman aboard it had sparked something in him as no woman had for years. But, swinging his horse in the direction of the valley, Stavros also knew that if given the chance, he wouldn't do anything about it.

Or rather, he would.

He would steer clear of her.

Go in the opposite direction.

He didn't need a woman complicating his life, particularly not a woman who was obviously city born and bred. He'd been married to one of them.

He gently kicked his horse into a trot.

And she'd almost killed him.

Chapter 2—Mr. Tortoise

The village of Kastro sat gleaming in the sun like a necklace of rubies and pearls, and Allie didn't think the illustrator of *Collection of Classic Fairy Tales* had portrayed his fictitious mountain village to be nearly as charming as this one was. Not only was it topped by the castle she had already fallen in love with, but it came complete with a Byzantine church and little streets and alleyways that climbed the steep mountainside with a grace that only very old towns can wear.

Entering the village, Allie glimpsed vine-covered verandas and rose-filled gardens with sweeping eucalyptus and modest citrus trees peeking out from behind old garden walls. It was spotless, and by the time the bus pulled up into the shaded village square, Allie had lost her heart to Kastro.

People gravitated to the bus like thirsty animals to a spring. Allie was surprised by how many people there were. Glancing at her watch, she saw it was almost siesta time, an institution in the villages of Greece. But still, men ambled out from the village *kafenion*—coffee shop—women wiping their hands on aprons appeared from kitchens, and children ran from hidden playing fields, flushed and excited. Chatting animatedly, they all wanted to greet the bus, which brought a little bit of the outside world to Kastro three times a week.

Allie let out a contented breath. These were to be her people—to care for, to get to know, to live with as neighbors. She had heard that villagers treated doctors who were a part of the Rural Physician Service as much-loved and respected members of the community. As she gathered her purse and medical bag, she knew that was yet another reason she had decided to become a country doctor. She wanted to be a member of a tight-knit, family-type community. Her fun-loving mother had died when she was only eight, and her dear but serious father ten years later. The only family Allie had now was her beloved brother, Alex, who was a US Navy Seal and deployed in a place he couldn't even tell her about.

Anticipating a good welcome, she felt a smile touch her face as she alighted from the bus. But when the soles of her sandals touched the ground, all talking stopped with the finality of a TV being switched off, as everyone, from the oldest of men to the youngest of children, turned to stare at her.

Allie felt her skin suffuse with color. Certain, though, that once they knew who she was she would be welcomed, and grandly, Allie shifted her medical bag in front of her. Speaking in Greek, which had become, after her years in medical school, almost another native language, she introduced herself. "Hello. I'm Allie Alexander. Your new doctor."

From everything she had heard, that news should have been greeted enthusiastically.

But it wasn't.

If anything, it made the quiet even quieter. Now even the old men's *komboloi*—worry beads—stopped their rhythmic *click, click, click*, while the stare of many became as one.

Feeling confused, Allie asked, "This *is* the village of Kastro, isn't it?" But she was certain it was. The castle, *kastro*, sitting on the mountaintop above, proclaimed the village's name.

When the villagers remained silent, the bus driver looked up from pulling her suitcases out of the luggage compartment and answered her. "Sure is." Even he looked bewildered by their lack of welcome.

Allie nodded her thanks to him before further inquiring of the silent crowd, "Kastro is the seat of the medical clinic for this area, isn't it?"

After a very long pause, a giant of a man wearing a shirt that had matching sweat marks of huge diameter under each armpit, swaggered to the front. With eyes small and mean, he drawled out, "It is. But you're not welcome here."

Allie blinked. "I beg your pardon?"

"I said," he repeated as if she were dense, "you are not welcome here." From the gloating way his eyes met his cronies', she knew he was drawing strength from the embarrassment and confusion with which his words were meant to fill her. But Allie had seen his type before—a person who grew bigger as he hurt and oppressed others—and she had had it.

She might like fairy tales and dreams of a perfect land, and it might have been nice to have been welcomed, if not profusely then at least civilly. But more than anything else, Allie was a pragmatist. The events in her life had formed her into a person who could be as stubborn and as determined as the best of them.

Sending all fanciful thoughts back to storybooks where they belonged and not giving the man or the people who hovered behind him like zombies from the *Twilight Zone* another glance, she left her luggage under the huge plane tree and marched into the *kafenion* that opened onto the square.

She was hot.

She was tired.

And she was thirsty.

Before she took another step or said another word, she was going to get an ice-cold cola.

The *kafenion* was dingy, but its thick stone walls kept it refreshingly cool. A woman came out from behind a curtained-off area, the clicking of her dentures proclaiming her presence. Not even the fact that she was as sour-faced as a prune—and Allie knew she could expect no welcome from her, either—could deter Allie from getting that drink.

"One cola please," she ordered, and, reaching into her purse, she placed its cost upon the scarred wooden table.

Allie heard the shuffling sound of people following her in, and from the corner of her eye, she saw the ponderous bulk of the man whom she now thought of as the ogre leading the way. The woman behind the counter darted a nervous glance in his direction, not even trying to hide from Allie the tilt of her head as she silently asked his permission to serve the drink.

Allie's gaze swiveled to meet his as she dared him to say no.

He shrugged his bulky shoulders and nodded to the woman. Clicking her ill-fitting teeth loudly, the woman turned and went into the back area.

While Allie waited for the cola, she didn't look to the right or to the left. When the woman returned and plopped the drink in front of her, Allie drank it all down before she turned to face the villagers again.

The men, that is.

With the exception of the prune-faced woman, all the women and children had disappeared. A glance out the door revealed the square to be empty, too. Allie remembered hearing that in the more remote areas, the village *kafenion* was a male stronghold. She just hadn't believed it. Until now.

Taking a deep breath, she addressed the "Men's Club." "Someone can either show me to the medical clinic—or I will find it myself."

When all their gazes shifted toward the ogre, Allie's did, too. Without flinching a muscle, she informed him, "I have the key."

The Department of Health had given it to her in the city. She was glad that they had had such foresight.

There was a charged moment before the ogre commanded the woman behind the counter, "Dionysia. Take her."

From the smirking stretch of his thick lips, Allie had the unsettled feeling he hid something, but with a confidence to her steps that held no hesitation or weakness, she followed the scowling woman out the door and across the square to a winding lane.

If circumstances had been different, Allie would have enjoyed the walk. Eucalyptus trees lined the way, with walnut, olive, and citrus groves appearing in the distance. Some houses were old, some were new, but they all had one thing in common: They were all kept in beautiful shape.

Except for one: the small whitewashed building with the official blue and white sign designating it as belonging to the Department of Health.

It wasn't that its paint was peeling or that its shutters were sagging, but rather, it had an unkempt, abandoned air about it. Like the overgrown rosebushes under its shuttered windows, it simply needed care. For the first time, Allie wondered how long Kastro had been without a doctor and why.

Smacking her dentures together, the woman named Dionysia pushed open the door with a reverberating bang. With a surly look in her washed-out eyes, she stood back for Allie to be the first to enter the dark interior of the building.

Taking a deep breath, Allie reached for the light switch. But even before her fingers found it, her nose warned her that all was not going to be as it should. Mustiness and neglect clung to the air, as it would to a dungeon.

Allie flipped on the lone light bulb and gasped.

23

The room, which Allie supposed was the waiting area, was a mess. It looked as though it hadn't seen a broom or a mop in at least a year. Papers littered the floor, while intricate spider webs hung like eerie wall hangings in the corners and in the niches around the windows. The sofa was turned on its side, and the wicker in the chairs had unraveled.

There was a closed door at the other end of the room, which Allie assumed led to her living quarters. But first, wanting to see the entire clinic, she crossed to the examining room, hoping she would find better conditions there.

But if anything, it was worse.

Medical equipment had been left lying around the room, with used wads of bloodstained cotton balls sitting in soiled trays and in the small metallic sink. The examining table was torn, and her desk had broken ampoules of medicine littering its stained wood, while the medicine cabinet's glass doors were too covered with grime to see through.

Allie reached for the handle and pulled it open. A scorpion—a little larger than an old silver dollar—ran from a length of unwound gauze and up the side of the peeling chest.

"Eek!" Allie yelled and dropped her hand, both instinctive gestures. She turned to the woman beside her, but when the woman only grunted, and in a pleased sort of way, Allie thought it best to ignore her.

Envisioning creepy crawly things running all over her skin, but striving not to show it, Allie left the medicine chest to the scorpion and walked over to a row of boxes that were, surprisingly, covered by a protective tarpaulin. They were the only things that seemed to be cared for in the building.

Pulling back the cover carefully so that the mice droppings that dotted the top would not fall on her, Allie was amazed to discover about twenty boxes of medical equipment and supplies stacked underneath.

She checked the transfer dates. They had arrived within the last month. For the first time since meeting the people of Kastro, Allie smiled. She knew that with these supplies, she could put together a decent medical station.

Pulling a tissue from her purse, she dusted off her hands and, turning to the woman, asked, "Who's in charge of cleaning the clinic?" Allie thought it was a reasonable question, a logical one. But the woman didn't seem to think so. Making a sound that resembled a pig snorting, she turned on her small feet and shuffled out of the building.

"Whew boy," Allie sighed out and watched the woman disappear down the walkway before she let her gaze wander again around the dusty, disheveled interior of the clinic. "Lord?" she asked of the only One who had never let her down. "It is Your will for me to be here, isn't it?"

Shaking her head, she went to the window behind the desk, and, to a rain of chipped paint and dust falling on and around her, she pulled it open. Coughing, she waved the dust away from her face while she reached for the shutters. She was amazed when they easily swung outward.

The view from the window made her forget the mess she had landed herself in. Red and yellow roses with an occasional pink one scented the air, while the green-and-golden patchwork valley shimmered far below. A scratching sound on the ground brought Allie's gaze downward.

She gasped in pleasure.

A tortoise, probably the largest Allie had ever seen, was sunning itself below the rosebush. Its head was tilted upward, and its beady little eyes, the friendliest ones Allie had encountered in the village thus far, were blinking up at her, while its tongue moved in and out of its mouth like a toothless old man trying to form his words.

Looking at that big, beautiful land turtle, Allie knew he was a direct sign from God, a sign telling her better than a million words ever could that in spite of her reception in the village, in spite of the disrepair of the clinic, she was right where she was supposed to be, right where God would have her. Because more than any other of God's creatures, turtles were Allie's love. Sea turtles, land turtles, even snapping turtles, Allie loved all members of the Testudinata family. She hadn't been allowed a dog or a cat in New York City, but her father had always allowed her a turtle. She had cried very sad tears when her little turtle had died a few years back.

But now, in her new home of Kastro, God had sent her a new one: a great big new one, and laughter, her mighty laughter, which her brother always said gave the word *delight* voice, rose from within her to spill out over the Hellenic countryside. "Hello, Mr. Tortoise," she greeted it after a moment. "Have you come to welcome me?"

The turtle blinked up at Allie again, and she was sure he was grinning at her. His presence made turning back to the unsightly disorder behind her easier.

But as her gaze traveled around the depressing room, she sighed. Never in her dreams—and Allie had had many of them—had she imagined that she would find such conditions in Kastro.

But with a firm flick of her right braid, knowing that she had to get herself settled before she tackled the office, she walked over to the far door she had seen in the waiting room. She wondered in what sort of state she might find the doctor's quarters. Would it be asking too much to find a snug little apartment with a vine-laden veranda for the fragrant days of summer and a sturdy little fireplace to keep her warm in the winter?

Taking an anticipatory breath, she opened the door.

Not to the expected apartment, but rather, to the great outdoors and—to a donkey!

A donkey who seemed right at home in what Allie quickly realized was the backyard of the clinic. But even more, a donkey who seemed none too pleased at having her siesta interrupted!

Slamming the door shut, Allie leaned her back protectively against it while her gaze swiveled frantically around the room for another door. But there wasn't one, and she knew that there wasn't one in the examining room either.

Only the two rooms made up the clinic.

There wasn't even a bathroom.

Expelling a disappointed sigh, Allie Alexander, M.D., had no idea where she was supposed to live.

No idea at all.

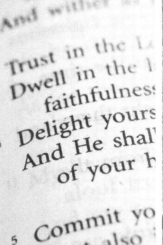

And wither as

Trust in the L
Dwell in the l
faithfulness
Delight yours
And He shal
of your h

5 Commit yo
also

Chapter 3—Papouli

With a decisive motion, Allie reached for her purse and medical bag and set off back toward the *kafenion*. Determination and unshakable courage to face a situation, no matter how unpleasant, flowed through her, as adrenaline pumped through her system. It was a feeling with which not only her work but also her life had given her experience in coping.

Squaring her shoulders, she braved the "Men's Club" once again. She paused just inside the door as all the normal café noises—the shuffling of playing cards, the clicking of worry beads, the clattering of dice against wooden backgammon boards—ceased. That her presence in the *kafenion* disturbed the men was obvious. That she didn't care was readily apparent to them, as, with a slight, defensive tilt of her jaw—one she was very aware of—she walked to a table and, pulling out a wooden chair, sat down.

When the sour-faced woman poked her head out from behind the curtained-off area, Allie immediately ordered another ice-cold cola. The woman quickly plopped the drink in front of her. Disregarding the proprietress, just as she did the men, Allie wrapped her fingers around the coolness of the bottle, placed her lips over the straw that danced around its opening, and slowly—very, very slowly this time—sipped the sweet, bubbly liquid.

The ticking of the 1950s Coca-Cola clock on the wall behind the cash register was the only noise in the room, and as the moments mounted one upon the other, it seemed to sound louder and more insistent, until the ogre finally slammed the front legs of his chair down onto the stone floor.

"We weren't expecting a woman doctor!" he fired out into the charged atmosphere. And as the men around him mumbled, like sheep bleating in a barnyard, that they hadn't been expecting a woman, either, Allie thought she just might have been given the reason for their antagonism.

Because she was a woman.

But she wasn't sure.

Nagging doubts made her think that there was more to it than simple gender prejudice.

Not even bothering to address his comment, Allie drew in another deep sip of soda before asking, "Where do Kastro's doctors normally live?"

"Well," the hulking man drawled out, "they normally live in the schoolteacher's house." He paused and smiled so broadly that Allie could see a couple of gold teeth in the back of his mouth. "But you can't."

Not a flicker of emotion showed in Allie's face as she asked, "And why is that?"

"Because you're a woman," he stated as if that explained everything.

Allie knew very well that she was a woman, and she was beginning to get a little tired of being reminded of it by this poor excuse of a man. Standing, she sipped the last drop of cola, placed the bottle back on the table, and said, "Well, I'll talk to the teacher and see what he has to say about it."

"Can't," the ogre returned smugly, and Allie knew from the way he shuffled the cards in his paw-like hands so confidently that the game he was playing with her wasn't over yet. "The teacher's not in town," he said, and fear that the teacher might not return until school started in four weeks' time radiated through Allie. If that was the case, she wasn't sure what she was going to do. Maybe start searching for a fairy godmother? The whimsical side of her answered the practical, and she was glad she could still have such frivolous thoughts while her immediate future seemed so uncertain.

"Then I'll talk to him when he returns," she stated, and nodding curtly to the men, she walked toward the exit.

"Nope. You can't live with him," the ogre's nasal voice followed her. "People will talk. You know…a single man…a single woman…living in the same house…" He let the insinuation breed in the air, even as the words came out of his mouth. From her peripheral vision she saw the other men nod their heads as they agreed that people would certainly "talk."

But without breaking her pace, without letting a single muscle in her body convey that she had caught his ugly innuendo, she continued toward the door.

But she had caught it.

A perfect catch, in fact.

In light of what she had gone through a few months before with the soccer star, she inwardly cringed.

"Can't have no hanky-panky going on between our doctor and teacher, now can we?" Allie heard the ogre plant the seed of rumor deeper into the dirt of the village as her feet took her out into the now-empty square.

She was angry. She was disappointed. But more than anything, she was disgusted with herself and her fairy-tale notions. She knew the beauty of the land, the castle, and then seeing a man who could be any woman's idea of a prince had her forgetting the other ingredients that made up fairy tales.

Wicked stepmothers, witches, and ogres…

She sighed. In that case, didn't there have to be a fairy

godmother around somewhere?

She shook her head as the verses from Psalm 37—real words of wisdom to live by—went through her head. "Trust in the Lord and do good; dwell in the land and enjoy safe pasture. Delight yourself in the Lord and he will give you the desires of your heart. Commit your way to the Lord; trust in him and he will do this: He will make your righteousness shine like the dawn, the justice of your cause like the noonday sun."

Smiling as the verses of promise sank into her being, Allie swept her gaze over the still village and reminded herself that most of the villagers had not been about when she'd arrived. It was siesta time, the hottest time of the day, and most were quite wisely escaping the heat by sleeping. Surely when others appeared, a house or a room for her to rent could be found.

She sank onto the largest of her suitcases and rubbed her hand across her hot forehead. She wished that she could sleep, too. The emotions and physical work involved with making this move had caught up with her, and all she wanted was to lie down under the coolness of the reaching plane tree and let sleep overtake her.

With the cicadas seeming to serenade her, the broad trunk of the old tree welcoming her head, and the heated air surrounding her like a down comforter, she felt, in spite of the hostility she had encountered, safe, and her eyes closed. She dozed. She didn't know for how long—it couldn't have been more than a minute or two—but when her lids slowly parted, she thought she was dreaming.

Before her, wearing a long robe with a matching black cap and with a long gray beard that had probably been only slightly trimmed in his entire life, stood a man with the kindest set of eyes Allie had ever seen.

"Well, well...could this Sleeping Beauty be Kastro's new doctor?" the man asked, his voice deep and gravelly and very, very friendly.

Allie smiled sheepishly, and he laughed, a good sound that brought all the fairy-tale wonder of the land back into Allie's heart, and she knew she must be looking at the village priest. But at the moment he seemed more like a fairy godfather.

Pulling herself away from the tree trunk, she stood. Just a little taller than her five feet five inches, the priest was thin and as spry as a young boy. Allie didn't think he could be a day over sixty, and yet, at the same time, he seemed ageless. She extended her hand to him. "I'm Allie Alexander, and I am Kastro's new doctor."

He took her hand in his, a callused one, Allie noticed, and she knew this was no idle priest. "And I'm Theodore Pappas. Welcome, *Yatrinna*."

His use of the term *yatrinna* brought an unexpected burst of gratification to Allie. Meaning "lady doctor," it was used by country folk as a sign of respect for a female doctor's professional standing. After her lack of welcome, it was wonderful to be so addressed, and by the priest, the most respected person in village communities.

"Thank you, Papouli." She returned the honor by calling him a "grand-fatherly" priest, and his smile widened, and she knew he liked it.

"But why are you sleeping here in the square?" His eyes danced in merriment behind his wire-framed glasses. "Why are you not in the apartment that has been made ready for you?"

Lines of puzzlement crisscrossed her brow. That there was a place prepared for her was news to her. "Papouli..." She paused and licked her lips, not sure how to continue. She was a stranger, and the people of this village were both his family and his flock. She didn't want to complain about people he had probably known all his life or want him to think she was a whining baby.

But Theodore Pappas was a priest who knew human character well, and his wise old eyes easily registered that something was amiss. "Please, feel free to tell me anything," he urged, and she saw him then as a man of God, in the truest and most unadulterated form.

So Allie told him. "I'm afraid the people, the men," she amended and motioned toward the *kafenion*, "have made it quite clear that there is nowhere for me to live in this village."

"Bah." The priest's deep, gravelly voice bayed in perfect synchronization with his eyebrows shooting up above the rim of his glasses. "Nowhere for you to live? But you will live where all the other doctors have lived—in the schoolteacher's house." He answered his own question as if it were a foregone conclusion.

"But they said that since I'm a woman—" She let the rest of the sentence trail off.

"Bah." He cut in authoritatively and guided her toward the *kafenion* door. "Come. I will set everything straight."

Chapter 4— Byzantine Chalet

And Papouli did.

Like a fairy godfather with a magic wand, he cast a spell of goodness, or at least one of compliance, over everyone in the *kafenion*. They all sat up a bit straighter when Papouli entered the room, and when Allie came in behind him in his respectful wake, their gazes shifted to meet one another, like children caught doing something wrong. Allie wasn't surprised to see that even the ogre held Papouli in esteem.

"Does anyone have any objections to our yatrinna living in the teacher's house?" he asked without preamble, and his sharp eyes, peering above the rims of his glasses, touched on everyone in the *kafenion*. When no one spoke up, not even the ogre, Papouli dismissed the subject with a slight "harrumph," and after instructing two of the men to carry Allie's luggage, he escorted her up through the winding lanes of the shuttered village to a beautiful white house—one of fairy-tale proportions—that sat in the shadow of the castle directly above it.

Trailing Papouli into a courtyard that had the fragrance of summer hanging softly over it, she forced her tired body to follow him up the marble stairs and around the wraparound veranda, past an opaque glass door and several windows to a large wooden door at the far end of the back of the house. He pushed it open, and Allie's eyes widened at the beautiful apartment. Like a Byzantine chalet, it was of deep rich wood with old stone walls, with cushions and needlepoint pillows of bold colors highlighting it.

Allie stepped onto the polished, planked floor and felt as though she had walked into another era. Placing her medical bag by the antique desk that was to her left, her gaze ran over the wood-based sofa that sat in an L shape in front of a lovely *tzaki*—fireplace—the focal point of the traditional room. A breakfast bar backed the shorter part of the sofa, and a galley kitchen was behind it, the modern appliances all artfully hidden below. A brick wall with wooden shelves of the same dark wood as the shutters made up the other side of the kitchen. Ceramic jugs, bowls, and plates of earth tones, which she knew had to be antiques, lined the shelves.

She walked behind the brick wall and into the sleeping area. A huge wardrobe stood to the left, but it was the raised platform bed that drew the attention of her drooping eyes. It was covered with the same ecru fabric that was on the sofa, with colorful throw pillows on top, and she couldn't resist trying it out. She sat on the edge. The mattress was firm but soft—exactly as she liked it. Looking across the room, she watched in wonder as the priest directed the men to place her luggage next to the fireplace. So much had changed since meeting Papouli—that wonderful man of God. Both relief and amazement filled Allie.

The priest turned to her, and his brows rose above his glasses as a look of satisfaction covered his face. "Ah, Yatrinna. You like your new home?"

Sweeping her gaze up at the beamed ceiling and then out through the French doors at the fabulous view of the valley and of the tall mountains beyond, Allie felt tears prick the back of her eyes. After the way she had been treated, and after seeing the mess her office was in, the joy she felt over meeting the priest and being brought to this charming abode was almost overwhelming. She wondered at the extremes she had met in the village.

Fairy tale, indeed.

It had all the makings of a classical one.

She stood, then walked over to the desk and slid her fingers over the ancient Byzantine icons that hung to its side. "I love it, Papouli," she murmured.

"Good," he said and turned toward the door. "I will leave you to rest, and this evening you will come to dinner at my house. It's the house with blue door next to the church," he proclaimed in a way that brooked no arguments, and turning, he briskly strode out the door.

Allie ran after him, but she was only in time to see the hem of his robe as it followed him around the veranda's corner. She could hear his spry steps as he bounded down the stairs. Smiling warmly, she turned back to the apartment, and leaving the door open to create a crosscurrent, she went over to the sofa and folded herself into its welcoming comfort.

Leaning her head back, her gaze roamed over the huge tzaki, with its arched arms that extended out of the wall, before her eyes settled on the ceramic vase that was full to overflowing with wild, cut roses that decorated the summertime hearth. The roses filled the apartment with their welcoming bouquet. Allie closed her eyes and breathed in deeply of the soft, natural fragrance. It filled her senses, calmed her mind. That a man whom she had never met had gone to such trouble to have such a beautiful residence all ready for her arrival touched a deep part of her soul, a part that hadn't been touched in a very long time. Not since her father had been alive had anyone done kind little things for her. Somehow it made her feel safe.

Standing, she stretched her arms above her head, hoping to feed strength back into her blood. But it didn't do any good. She was exhausted. She needed sleep.

Of their own volition, her fingers nimbly undid her braids. She pulled her sleeping mask from her purse then stumped on legs that were almost too heavy to carry her any farther over to the sleeping alcove. Lowering her weary body onto the inviting bed, she pulled her mask over her eyes and was asleep almost before her head fell against the softness of the pillow. Asleep in a land of castles and of fairy godfathers, where a prince with dark eyes sat on a horse of the most pure white, a horse that seemed to *clip-clop* around in her head…

***

"Who are you, and what are you doing in my house?" The demand punctured the sweetness of Allie's sleep like a bubble being popped. She pushed her sleeping mask up and willed her lids to lift their slumbering weights from her vision.

But when she did, she wondered if she were only dreaming of being awake.

She seemed to be floating, and everything seemed unreal and foggy. But more than that, the prince of her dreams, who had somehow acquired the same features as the man on the horse—whom she had seen while on the bus—was leaning over her.

Groggily, she gazed up his shirt to his strong chin and past his chiseled nose. When her gaze collided with his—hard and dark—he demanded again, "I asked who are you, and what are you doing in my house?" Allie felt less like a princess and more like Goldilocks of the Three Bears fame, with the man before her being the angry papa bear. She wished that she could get up and run away home like that heroine had. But she couldn't. She was at home.

"Baba..." the girl-cub by his side, who was the image of him, admonished with preadolescent embarrassment. Her brown eyes were trained on Allie, too, but unlike her father's, they held wonder and friendship in their remarkable depths.

Allie smiled at her, but when her fingertips ran across the fabric beneath her and she realized where she was—flat on her back in bed—she shot up, swung her feet to the side, and stood, ignoring the pounding in her head that was unprepared for such an abrupt change. "Hi," Allie addressed the girl, her friendly eyes preferable to those of her papa.

"Hi," the girl immediately returned, and Allie could see thrilled curiosity nearly ready to burst from her. "Are you the new doctor?" the girl asked with hope in her voice.

"I am." Allie couldn't help smiling at the excitement that was barely contained in the girl's compact body as she swiveled to her father.

"See, Baba...I told you," she squealed out her delight.

Allie saw lines of incredulity slash across the man's broad forehead as he looked at her above his daughter's head. *"You* are the new doctor?" It was more an accusation than a question.

Remembering their encounter on the bus, Allie understood his trepidation, and reluctantly, hesitantly, she nodded her head. The tightening of his jaw told her that he was remembering their first meeting, too. And with the same discomfort. She had liked the idea of romance with this man when he had been a stranger on a horse going in the opposite direction, but now that he was probably the man in whose house she was to live, well, it was a possibility she wouldn't even consider. Her professional integrity was too important to her for that.

"And you..." Her throat had gone totally dry. Clearing it, she started again. "I mean, you aren't by any chance the schoolteacher, are you?" But even as she asked, she knew he was. The ogre had led her to believe that the schoolteacher was going to be out of town for quite some time, not just hours. Obviously, he had meant to mislead her in the hopes that she would get on the next bus—or donkey—heading out of town.

"I am," he confirmed, his voice low, like the distant rumble of a dangerous thunderstorm.

"Oh," was all Allie said as attraction ricocheted between them. Something alive, something demanding, it rebounded between him and her, looking for a place to land. But that was not something she desired. She was thankful he seemed to feel the same way.

Trying to cover her reaction with a businesslike approach, she offered her hand to him and introduced herself. "I'm Allie Alexander."

With his deep eyes regarding her, measuring her, she lifted her chin and measured him back. Silently, communicating on a level that had no need for words, they agreed not to comment on the emotion that was between them. The pact was made in the narrowing of their eyes, in the flaring of their nostrils, in the beating of their hearts.

But putting her hand in his, she couldn't pretend not to feel the wonder of his touch. From the way his eyes widened and brightened, he couldn't, either. Charged with magic, the touch was potent, and they let go of one another as if zapped.

"I'm Stavros Andreas," he quickly replied, turning to the girl by his side. "And this is my daughter, Jeannie."

Allie smiled at the girl, glad that she was with them, especially glad that she lived in the same house. "Hi again, Jeannie."

"Wow!" Jeannie clapped her hands together. "You're the

new doctor! You're going to live here!"

"No." Stavros's voice boomed, and both Allie and Jeannie turned to him. Allie knew that the features of their faces wore the same covering. Surprise. What amazed her, though, was that the schoolteacher's did, too. He seemed to be surprised by his own response even as he continued with, "I'm afraid that will be impossible."

"Excuse me?" Allie asked. After Papouli's assurances, this was the last thing she had expected.

"Baba...?" his daughter asked, and Allie could tell that she was as confused by his declaration as was she.

"It won't work out," he said, and like a general having issued an unpopular command, he turned on his heels and walked purposefully into the living area.

Allie and Jeannie followed him. Jeannie turned beseeching, puppy-dog eyes to Allie, a look that told Allie that the girl wanted her to live in the house just as badly as she wanted to. It gave Allie courage. It was wonderful to feel wanted, if only by a young girl.

"Mr. Andreas," Allie began to his solid back, "Papouli brought me here. He said all the doctors have lived here."

"They have." Jeannie's head bobbed up and down.

Stavros turned to face Allie. He didn't even try to deny it. "They have also all been men." His gaze swept over her face. "You're a woman."

Allie rolled her eyes and made an exasperated sound. "I have been of the female gender for all of my twenty-eight years. Why is it that everyone in this village feels as though they have to remind me of it?"

His brows cut an ambiguous line across his face. "What do you mean?"

43

Allie let out a vexed sound. "Let's just say the men in the *kafenion* weren't very pleased with the idea of Kastro having a female doctor."

His dark eyes narrowed, as though he was considering something. But he only said, "I wouldn't jump to conclusions, Doctor, if I were you."

"Jump to—" Allie stared at him, appalled by the idea. "Mr. Andreas, one thing I never do is 'jump to conclusions.' But when I'm told outright that I'm not wanted here and that the people weren't expecting a 'woman' doctor, what else am I to think?"

For a moment Allie thought he was going to say something, to shed some light on the unusual situation she had found waiting for her in Kastro. But he didn't, and when a deep breath came out instead of the words of enlightenment he might have spoken, Allie felt impotent to retrieve them.

Taking his daughter's hand, he crossed over to the front door, which was still as Allie had left it before she fell asleep— wide open. "I'm sorry," he tossed over his shoulder, "but you will have to find other accommodation."

"But, Baba." Jeannie pulled on his hand, forcing her father to stop and turn around. "Didn't you tell me yesterday, while we were picking the flowers"—she pointed to the summer bouquet that sat tellingly on the hearth—"that there is no place else for the doctor to live?"

"Jeannie." It was a command such as parents give to their children the world over. It meant "be quiet." Jeannie recognized it and obeyed.

"I'm sorry," the girl mumbled and lowered her eyes while her ears turned red with embarrassment. Allie's heart went out to her. Her father wasn't being fair to her.

Stavros sighed, and as he gazed at his daughter's bent head,

Allie knew this was a parent who loved his daughter very much and would do almost anything for her. That he felt bad about his reaction was evident in the emotions that skipped across his face.

She watched as he placed his left hand in his pocket and jiggled some coins together for a few seconds. Allie couldn't help but feel as though he was weighing the possibility of her staying. But if that was the case, when he turned to her, she knew from his guarded expression that she had come up short on the scales.

"I'm really sorry. But I don't think Kastro's the place for you. It's remote, with problems a city person can't even imagine," he insisted.

But Allie wasn't about to give up. He might sound definite, but trained as she was in reading symptoms in patients, she saw the battle within, the hesitancy, even, in his stance. She knew how to use that knowledge. "Mr. Andreas, I signed a year-long contract with the Department of Health to be this village's doctor. I will complete the year even if I have to live in the clinic and sleep on the examining table to do so."

Jeannie's distraught brown-eyed gaze shot upward to her father's. "But she can't live there! It doesn't even have a tzaki for the winter. Baba…" she implored, and Allie could tell the teacher was startled at how badly his daughter wanted her—the doctor—to live in their spare apartment. Allie couldn't help but wonder where the girl's mother was. The men at the *kafenion* had said that the schoolteacher was single. Did that mean he was divorced or a widower?

Allie watched as his eyes took on a soft light as he regarded his daughter, and seeing it, Allie knew that the girl was the most important person in his life. She knew because her own father used to look at her and her brother in the same way.

45

"Jeannie," he spoke gently, "please go to your room until I call you. I would like to speak with the doctor alone."

Shoulders slumped, Jeannie lowered her head, and walking over to the wooden door that was situated to the right of the desk, the girl turned the handle, opened it, and disappeared through it. Allie's eyes widened.

She looked at the girl's father in bewilderment, something she wasn't used to feeling. "I thought...I mean...I assumed...isn't that the bathroom?"

"It is," he answered, totally perplexing Allie.

She opened her mouth to asked what he meant, but closed it on the question. She wasn't sure she wanted to know.

"That's the reason you can't live here."

"What do you mean?"

He walked over and opened the door wide. "Our apartments are connected by this central hall," he said and pointed out the area.

Allie poked her head in to inspect it. He flipped on the antique wooden chandelier that hung from the center, and she saw the hall had three doors opening off it.

"We can lock our doors," Allie said, with what she thought was total logic. "It's just like living in an apartment complex."

"Except"—with the flourish of a real estate agent showing a room, he swung open the middle door—"we share the house's only bathroom."

Chapter 5 — The Bathroom

So?" she couldn't help asking. To her mind it was similar to sharing a bathroom in a coed dorm.

"So I just can't see myself sharing a bathroom."

"But why?"

He let out a deep breath and ran his hand through his hair, rumpling it. "Look. You might be from the city and think in very modern terms, but I just don't. I don't like the idea of sharing my bathroom with you, a woman."

Allie suspected that neither the fact that she was from the city nor that she was a woman was really the problem. The problem was the way the woman in her encountered the man in him to make them aware of one another in a way that scared them both.

She had seen fear in patients' faces enough times to recognize that was what Stavros Andreas was feeling. She felt it, too. As much as she would like a man in her life, she didn't want a relationship with a man in whose house she rented an apartment. She glanced toward the bathroom.

Trying to buy some time, she asked, "Umm, do you mind if I wash my hands? I haven't had a chance since arriving in the village."

He cleared his throat in an awkward way and took a step back. "Not at all."

"May we finish talking in a few moments?"

"I don't see that we have much more to say to one another."

"I believe we do."

He shrugged his shoulders. "Come on over to my apartment

after you've freshened up." Turning, he opened the door she supposed his daughter had gone through a few moments before and went in, shutting it with a small click.

Allie sighed and walked into the bathroom. Of marble and wood, it was anything but traditional. It was modern and spotless and like those one might find in a penthouse on Park Avenue in New York City.

"The man likes his comforts," Allie mumbled to her reflection as she turned on the tap and washed her hands and face to the hum of a pump. But she had to admit that she was glad that he did. A nice bathroom was about the only thing Allie had dreaded not finding in a remote village. She had heard that in some villages the doctors still had to deal with no indoor water and, horror of horrors, outhouses. . . .

She shuddered, and the thought that her clinic had only a sink, a very dirty, grimy one, and a donkey in the backyard where the outhouse was most likely located made her resolve to live in this house even stronger. Much stronger.

***

But the only thing Stavros had resolved as he stood staring out his kitchen window at the castle above was that Allie Alexander, M.D., couldn't live in his house.

When he had seen the open door of the spare apartment, the one which he and his daughter always referred to as "the doctor's apartment," the last thing he had expected to find was the beautiful woman who had occupied so much of his thoughts during the last few hours sleeping like a fairy princess on the bed.

It had thrown him.

The fact that she looked even more beautiful in repose, with her long hair gracefully settled around her head, brought a part of him to life that he thought he had successfully extinguished. All he had wanted to do was to lean over and kiss her full lips, to kiss her awake like he was Prince Charming himself.

He shook his head.

What was he thinking?

No, the lady could not live in his house. That was a definite.

Still, he wondered at how the first woman to really interest him since his wife was the very one who, by rights of her professional standing, should be allowed to live in the spare apartment. It had never even occurred to him that the woman he had seen through the open window of the bus could possibly be Kastro's new doctor.

He frowned. He couldn't ever remember any doctors he had ever visited being so beautiful. But he should have known who she was. Kastro was the terminus of the bus route. In the three years he had lived in the village, he had never seen her before. He had never even seen a picture of her as being a member of somebody's family.

He would have remembered if he had.

No, he couldn't let her live in his house. If he had his way, she wouldn't even live in Kastro. He had worked too hard to make a life for his daughter and himself, and he didn't want any woman destroying it. Especially not a city woman, a woman who would be here for a few months—a year at the most, if she were conscientious—then leave, leaving him behind to pick up the pieces of his emotions, and dry his daughter's tears. No. He couldn't do that. Not again.

"Baba…" Jeannie's voice broke into his thoughts, and he turned to see her standing hesitantly in the doorway of her bedroom, her little Siamese cat held comfortingly against her shoulder. Even after nine years, it still amazed Stavros to think that he had had a part in making her and that she was his daughter. He loved being her baba, her father. She made being a father wonderful.

He smiled and held out his arms to her. "Come here."

Grinning broadly, Jeannie put the cat down, then ran across the wooden floor into her father's waiting arms. "Oh, Baba… I love you."

"And I love you, pumpkin." Jeannie was the most important person in the world to him. He would do almost anything to give her a good life.

He had.

He'd given up a prestigious position as a university professor in the States to become a village schoolteacher so that he could raise her himself and not leave her in the care of a babysitter day after day until she was all grown up. It was a decision he had never regretted.

Her mother had deserted her.

He never would.

"Baba…" She let go of him to scoot up onto the kitchen counter. It had been Jeannie's place since long before they had moved permanently into what had been Stavros's ancestral home. They had used the old place as a summer vacation home—as had his parents before him—before renovating it and turning it into their permanent residence. He had brought Jeannie here every summer. Except for the first time, he and his daughter had come alone. His wife hadn't wanted any part of the pastoral village way of life after that first summer.

"What is it, pumpkin?" he prompted, although he knew what was on her mind.

"Please...please..." She squeezed her eyes together, as she always did when she really wanted something, before opening them wide again to finish her request. "Let the doctor live next door."

Stavros smiled. That was one of the many things he loved about being a father and about working with kids. He could always count on them to say exactly what was on their minds. The problem was that he didn't know how he could explain his reasons to her for not wanting the doctor to live in their house. Except for how attracted he was to the woman, he couldn't explain it to himself. And worse still, he knew that to use the bathroom as an excuse for the doctor not to live in the apartment was lame. Although the thought of her using the same bathtub he did bothered him. It was just too evocative.

Jeannie continued, obviously taking hope from the fact that he hadn't immediately said no. "I overheard you talking," she said, admitting to eavesdropping. "And I know you think the bathroom will be a problem." His smile deepened over her innocence in really believing that was the issue. "But we can work out a signal or something so that we know when it's being used," she completed with a logic for which Stavros couldn't help but be proud.

Reaching out, he undid her ponytail to fix the wisps of silky hair that had escaped it since that morning. "Why do you want her to live here?" he asked, really wanting to know.

"Because I like her. She's beautiful," Jeannie answered quickly, stating two reasons Stavros certainly couldn't deny. "And it's the doctor's apartment. The doctors *always* live here."

"True," he conceded, but as he pulled his daughter's thick hair through the band, he thought how the other doctors had not been beautiful young women. More particularly, one whom he felt mightily attracted to.

"And it's my turn to have a girl living next door," she continued, catching Stavros by surprise.

He looked at her in question. "What do you mean?"

"The other doctors have all been men like you. It's my turn to have one who's a woman."

Stavros twisted his lips in a playful way as he tapped his daughter on her nose. "Like you, you mean?"

"Ba...ba...like I will be," she said, and he could tell she was slightly exasperated that she had to clarify the obvious to him. Reaching up, she put both small hands on either side of his face, something she did when she really wanted him to pay attention to her. It forced him to look into her eyes. Brown ones, a shade lighter than his own. "Please, Baba. Please let her live with us!"

"Let her live with us..." Jeannie's words echoed in his brain, and Stavros thought again how innocent she was. He didn't know if he could give her what she wanted, but he was glad that, from all of this, he had learned how badly she wanted a woman around, wanted a mother around. It was a bittersweet knowledge, though, because a mother was the one thing Stavros didn't think he could give to her.

Not ever.

His wife's behavior had cut him deeply. Even after so much time, the emotional scar was still a red and oozing slash of bitterness and guilt across his cold heart—and it had only deepened when his wife had died recently while on a business trip, officially making him a widower. A true believer in the "until death do us part" section of the marriage ceremony, Stavros didn't think he could survive another relationship that might turn sour. Even more, he didn't want Jeannie to go through something like that. She had been too young to really understand that her mother hadn't wanted her, that the woman had deserted both of them upon the little girl's birth. At nine Jeannie could get hurt, really hurt. Something he couldn't, wouldn't, allow.

In spite of that totally male part of him that was urging him to get to know Allie Alexander better, he had to remind himself that the woman already had too many strikes going against her. She was an M.D., a professional, just like his wife, the lawyer, had been. And she was a city woman, again like his wife.

"Ba...ba..." Jeannie impatiently broke into his thoughts.

Removing his daughter's slender hands from his face, he murmured, "We'll see." That was all he could promise her. He was thankful that, for the moment, it seemed to be enough.

"Okay." She jumped down off the counter and ran over to the front door.

"Where are you going?" he asked. One of the many things he liked about village life was that it was a child's utopia. Everyone in the village looked out for one another's children. It was safe.

"Eva and I want to pick figs for Papouli. He likes the ones from our tree up by the spring." She reached for the basket that was kept handily by the door. "Besides"—she threw back over her shoulder—"don't you want to talk to the doctor. . .alone?"

Stavros's lips twisted in an amazed sort of way over his daughter's first attempt at matchmaking. But as she ran out the door and he turned back to gaze unseeingly at the stonework of the castle above his house, he knew from past experience that she was trying her hand at a match that could never work. He and professional women just didn't go together.

***

Allie turned the corner of the veranda just in time to see Jeannie's ponytail follow her with a jaunty bounce down the stairs.

She grimaced.

She had hoped the little girl would be present when she talked to Stavros Andreas. It might have been a cowardly desire, but Jeannie was a friend, something in short supply in this village, and Allie really liked the idea of the little girl becoming a regular visitor. Allie and children had always gotten along well, and she and Jeannie had clicked immediately.

Two swallows playing tag in the evening sky, with that same happy spirit that Allie loved in children, caught her attention. They led her gaze down to the blue-shuttered house that sat beside the Byzantine church midway down the village slope.

Papouli was another friend, and knowing he wanted her to live in the teacher's house made her resolve stronger. Nothing— not her racing heart, nor her fanciful thoughts, nor even the dark-eyed man who made her body react in a manner she never dreamed it could—was going to keep her from achieving her goals.

She would be cool and professional, and she would succeed.

Seeing that the door to the teacher's apartment was open, she took a deep controlling breath and poised her knuckles over the doorjamb to knock. But when she saw that Stavros Andreas was in the kitchen staring out the window, and that he hadn't seen her, her hand froze in midair even as her gaze roved over him.

He was tall, and every bit as princely as she had thought when she had seen him from the window of the bus. She decided she liked his hair and his hands the most. His hair was thick, falling recklessly across his cowlicked forehead as if he had just tamed a dragon, and his hands were long and broad and perfectly formed.

But spying on him wasn't cool. It made Allie feel anything but professional. She readied herself to knock again, but when the teacher whipped around quick as a sword flash to face her, Allie jumped back, startled.

The look plastered across his face made her feel as if she were a thief caught in the act of intruding. With sudden insight coming from years of dealing with people—people who had pains they could hardly explain—Allie knew he did consider her an intrusion in his life.

And that intrigued her.

***

Even though Stavros had been expecting her, it was a shock to actually see her standing at his door.

She had changed into a flowery sundress and summer shoes, flip-flops that showed the pink of her pretty polished toes. Her hair was back in the same double braids she had worn while on the bus, an elaborate concoction that he could never hope to achieve in Jeannie's hair. Normal braids he could handle. They were practical. This one wasn't. It was elegant and every bit as feminine as when her hair had been loose and mussed from sleeping. He liked the way it didn't hide her neck, her long, gently sloping neck. Her vulnerable neck.

That she was a stunning woman—at least to him—was obvious.

But it wasn't only that. Rather, it was that air she had about her, a grace, a class, and something else he couldn't quite place—

an inner sort of peace—that mixed with the determination in her eyes, with their softness, to present a woman whom—

Whom he couldn't let live in his house.

For one of the few times in his daughter's life, Stavros didn't think he could give Jeannie what she'd asked for.

When the doctor tilted her head upward and said in a formal and brisk take-charge manner, "Hello. May I come in?" it grated hard against Stavros's already taut nerves. It was the worst possible tone a woman could use with him. It smacked of his wife's snooty professional ways, and it not only irritated him but also brought all his apprehensions racing to the forefront of his mind. It made his resolve to prevent her from living in his house that much stronger. To get involved with another woman married to her career would be a big mistake.

One he couldn't make.

Walking around the kitchen bar, wanting only to conclude this interview as soon as possible, he motioned for her to enter and to be seated. "Please."

***

Sitting, Allie crossed her legs and glanced back up at him. But she quickly slid her gaze away. There was something about him that made her feel like a blushing adolescent. She hadn't felt this way since high school and Dale.

Dear Dale…a boy whose framed pictures had sat in every home, dorm, and apartment in which she had ever lived. Forever young, Dale's pictures would sit in the house next door, too. If it became her home.

Her gaze wandered and finally settled on the huge fireplace's hearth, with its bouquet of wild roses identical to the

58

welcoming ones in her apartment. She shifted her gaze to the medieval sword hanging over the mantle. Her lips curved slightly upward. But of course the prince had to have a sword. The whimsical part of her was never able to stay suppressed for long.

***

"May I get you something to drink or maybe some grapes and cheese?" Stavros asked. He might not want her here upsetting his life, but she had had a hard day, and he knew she must be in need of refreshment. Amazingly, his desire to see her gone fought with his desire to care for her, a desire that was growing stronger in him by the second as he watched the daisies on her dress move up and down with each breath she took and as the soft scent of her seemed to fill his house, his senses.

"Mr. Andreas, I would very much like to live here," she said, patting the sofa on which she sat. She cringed when his gaze fell to her hand.

"Would you?" he inquired, raising his eyebrows.

She gestured quickly with her upturned palm toward the other apartment. "I mean—"

"I know what you mean." He smiled. He was glad her slip had succeeded, at the very least, in diminishing the tension, which had spun around them like electrons in an atom.

Feeling relaxed for the first time since meeting her, he took the bowl of grapes from the counter and placed it on the coffee table before her. But he couldn't help but wonder if her slip had been a Freudian one, telling of what she really desired...

***

Allie was wondering the same thing. She didn't normally make such bloopers. Relieved to do something with her hands, she reached for a grape. Her teeth bit into it, and its sweet, refreshing juice was like nectar to her parched mouth, reminding her that to go to the Lord about this situation here and now would be like nectar to her soul.

Dear Lord, please help me say the right words.

Immediately, she felt the Spirit of God hug her close, as He had so many times in the past.

Feeling fortified, she glanced up at the schoolteacher and reached for another grape. "Mmm…they're delicious," she murmured.

"They're from my own vines."

"Really." Allie slanted him a glance, and interpreting his comment as friendly small talk—something hitherto totally lacking in their relationship—she quickly reciprocated. "That's one of the things I know I'll love about living in the country. It's so close to the real things in life, good things of the earth—"

"Dr. Alexander." There was no missing the annoyance that flickered across his face. "I don't think you appreciate what living in a village entails. There's a lot more to it than pretty hillsides and" —he waved his hand toward the bowl of grapes— "freshly picked fruit."

"Mr. Andreas, believe me, I know that. There's sickness and disease and"—she paused and gave a hesitant half smile— "houses without bathrooms." She hoped that he might respond to her gentle humor.

He didn't.

"There's that and much more," he agreed with a steely quality to his voice, one that brooked no attempt at friendliness. "Things you can't even imagine until you've lived here."

She sighed, and standing, walked over to the window. She glanced up at the strong walls of the castle before turning back to him. "Mr. Andreas, nobody forced me to come to Kastro. I wanted to come. I know there are things about village life I probably won't like. But there are things about city life I don't like, either." She waved her hand in dismissal of the subject, not knowing how much the confident gesture antagonized the man before her. "But that's not the issue. As I told you before, I signed a year-long contract, and I won't leave before it's up. My only problem now is finding a place to live."

***

Stavros was almost certain that wasn't going to be her only problem. During the three years he had lived in the village, he had come to the conclusion that Kastro's population was a microcosm of the world, with all the emotions of people contained within a few square miles. Right now there were problems brewing. Big ones. He suspected, too, that she knew it. Her lack of welcome had to have alerted her to it.

In spite of himself, a grudging respect for her was growing. He suspected that if he didn't let her live in his spare apartment, she would live at the clinic. He knew that Jeannie would never forgive him for that.

He continued to regard her.

She continued to regard him.

It was a showdown.

Finally, he motioned for her to sit back on the sofa. She went to it and sat.

Reaching next to him, he picked up one of his daughter's fashion dolls, and holding it between his fingers, he spoke. "I didn't realize how much my daughter misses having a woman around until...we found you sleeping next door."

"I'm sorry about that. If we—I mean—if I am to live here...there"—she motioned toward the other side of the house—"I'll be certain to close my door in the future."

He waved her apology aside. "It's not the first time I've seen a woman sleeping." But he knew from the soft blush that touched her face that she wasn't accustomed to men finding her in that kind of situation. The knowledge somehow pleased him. Especially since she was a professional woman. A part of him wondered if perhaps she was different, if it could work having her live in the doctor's apartment. For Jeannie's sake...

Coming to a sudden decision, he tossed the doll back onto the sofa and spoke before giving the rational part of his mind time to rule the irrational. "As you know, Jeannie wants you to live next door."

"Yes," she acknowledged and waited, and Stavros couldn't help but compare her quickly shining eyes with those of his daughter's. The color was different, but in many ways they were similar. Two girls hoping for something special, like a sleepover.

But there the resemblance ended. His feelings for this woman scared him. Scared him badly. But for Jeannie's sake, and even for this woman who seemed to be very nice—a nice woman who had no idea what she was letting herself in for in coming to Kastro—he thought he might be able to ignore his doubts.

School would be starting soon, and he would be busy. And she would be at the clinic most of the time. That fact would constantly remind him of what she was—a professional like his wife had been. A woman who had no room in her life for a family.

But this one would have to make room for Jeannie. He would make her living in the apartment contingent upon it. "Because of my daughter, we can try your living here." He waved his hand toward the other apartment, annoyed that he had made the same mistake as she. "I mean *there*. But I want Jeannie to be happy, to feel as though she has a friend in you." He paused. "Do I make myself clear?"

He watched as her eyes narrowed into a questioning frown. "Let me get this straight. What you're saying is that only if I am your daughter's friend will you let me live there?"

"That's right."

"Mr. Andreas, as I'm the one in need of friends here in Kastro, I'll be honored if your daughter counts me as one of hers."

"Good." That was all Stavros wanted to hear. He stood and held out his hand to her. "Then it's a deal." But when her hand touched his, he wasn't so sure if it was the right deal. Living with her under his roof and sharing the same bathroom might prove to be far more difficult in practice than in theory.

Stavros already regretted his moment of weakness.

***

But not Allie. She silently breathed out a prayer of thanks to God for softening this man's heart toward her.

She now had a home in Kastro.

Chapter 6—Martha & Natalia

The house with the blue door by the church housed one of the nicest families Allie had ever met. And in Papouli's daughters, Martha and Natalia, Allie found two more friends in Kastro.

"You don't know how glad we are that you've come to live here," Martha quickly said, as she placed a demitasse of fragrant Greek coffee on the patio table in front of Allie, amazing Allie at how fast she could do so without slopping any. A small woman full of joyful energy, Martha dressed as most village woman in a home-sewn skirt, a cotton t-shirt falling over its waist and slip-on leather shoes. Allie had quickly come to see that Martha was always in speedy motion, always doing something to make sure everyone around her was happy.

Her sister, Natalia, nodded in concurrence. "I don't feel so bad about leaving Baba"—the young woman's remarkable blue eyes glanced over at her father—"and Martha now that you're here."

Allie smiled at Natalia. She still couldn't help but be surprised by how she looked. When Papouli had first introduced his daughters, Allie had had to hide her shock at how different they were.

Martha was much shorter, a pretty woman whom Allie figured to be about forty, who greatly resembled her father. She kept her light brown hair, which in the early stages of turning a pretty gray, cropped close to her head. She was tidy and clean, didn't wear a stitch of make-up, and had probably never gone to a hairdresser in her life.

Natalia on the other hand, although following her sister in

her lack of make-up and zero time spent on a beauty routine, was dressed as younger women in the village were—summer jeans, a t-shirt tucked into her belted waist with Greek sandals covering her long slender feet. But unlike all other young women Allie had seen, she looked as though she had just stepped out of the pages of a fashion catalog. Natalia was stunning, made all the more so because she was completely oblivious to the rarity of her physical beauty, one Allie quickly realized was a mirror to that of her sweet soul.

After taking a sip of her thick, sweet coffee, Allie inquired of Natalia, "Are you looking forward to moving to Athens?"

"I can't wait!" the young woman exclaimed, the adventure of her move in her expressive eyes.

"Natalia has always wanted to go out into the world," Martha explained from her perch on the edge of her chair as she smiled fondly at her younger sister. "Our mother knew this even when Natalia was a little girl, and before she died, she made us"—she motioned between her father and herself—"promise that when the time came, we would let our Natalia go."

"Don't worry," Natalia whispered and reached first for her sister's and then for her father's hands, and Allie could feel the love that flowed between them. "I'll be back."

"You will follow the path God has laid out for you, my dear." Papouli patted his daughter's hand. "That is all I want for you."

"Dear Baba..." The young woman rubbed her father's callused hand against her smooth face. "You are the best father a girl could ever ask for."

Allie took another sip of coffee, and as the sounds of the summer night played around them—the click of a backgammon board at a neighboring house, dogs barking in the distance, a cricket in a walnut tree—Allie knew that she was witnessing a family as God intended. A family made up of members who loved and cared for one another.

Allie wished for such a family again. She and her brother, Alex, loved one another and had always been good friends but their father's death, coming right on the heels of Dale's, had been too much for him. Dale had been her brother's best friend and Alex had left home and joined the US military. Allie left home shortly afterward. Now they no longer even had a family house to call home. Looking at the three people before her, Allie hoped that Natalia and Martha would never drift apart.

"Are you going to be renting an apartment or living in a dorm?" Allie quickly asked, wanting to escape her thoughts. The family had told her earlier that Natalia was going to be attending an art school in Athens. Allie couldn't imagine the girl in anything other than arts.

"Oh, no. I'll be staying with my other sister."

"Your other sister?" Allie turned to Papouli in surprise. "I didn't realize that you had other children."

The priest's eyes twinkled as his gravelly voice proudly proclaimed, "I have six children. Three girls and three boys."

"And six grandchildren," Martha piped in.

"And two great-grandchildren!" Natalia finished.

"Papouli!" Allie was amazed. "That's wonderful!"

The older man beamed. "I love children. My wife was quite a bit older than me; otherwise we would have had more after Martha. Thankfully, Natalia came to us."

Allie looked from one to the other sister, and then she understood the difference in their appearance. "You mean—?"

"Our Natalia was a direct gift from God." Martha confirmed that Natalia had been adopted, as she squeezed her sister's long slender hand in her own much smaller one.

"One that came to us in a basket," Papouli qualified, and Allie could tell from the way his eyes narrowed and crinkled at the corners that he was remembering back to when his daughter had first come to him. "My wife had just learned that she had a very serious disease."

With a physician's interest, Allie tilted her head in question.

Papouli whispered the illness, and at Allie's look of understanding, he continued. "We were at the bus station waiting to return to Kastro. We were very sad, but all the while I was praying for a miracle. I was praying for God to somehow heal my dear wife, my dear Talia…" He looked over at Natalia and smiled with all the father's love a child could ever wish for shining in his wise eyes. "That was when I first heard Natalia cry. She was calling out to us."

"Someone had left her—a tiny little baby—in a basket at the bus station," Martha quickly explained, and Allie could hear the amazement in her voice, one that hadn't diminished with the years.

Papouli nodded. "No one came for her. We stayed in the town for a week looking for her parents—"

"But they couldn't find my parents," Natalia softly chimed in, finishing the story, one that almost seemed like a fairy tale to Allie. "Because my parents had just found me in that basket. No girl could ever ask to be part of a more wonderful family than this one."

Papouli smiled over at her. "God answered my prayer in our finding Natalia, too. The doctors thought that my wife wouldn't live more than a year or two. But because of Natalia, because Talia wanted to be a mother to her fair-haired child, she lived another ten years. Ten very wonderful years."

"So we don't feel as though we have the right to be sad in Natalia leaving us tomorrow." Martha finished the amazing story. "We look upon her being with us for the last eighteen years as a gift."

"And I believe"—Natalia reached across the circle of the wooden tabletop and tapped Allie on her arm—"that your coming to Kastro, Yatrinna, is a gift, too." At Allie's perplexed look, the blond beauty laughed, a laugh that sounded like crystal chiming in a gentle breeze, before she continued. "Even though I know that I have to go, I haven't liked the idea of leaving my sister and father. But now that you're here, I can leave knowing that Martha"—she looked over at her sister with a teasing glint in her eyes—"will have someone else to mother."

Allie turned estimating eyes to Martha. "I hardly think Martha is old enough to be my mother, Natalia," she murmured, feeling a bit uncomfortable for the older woman.

But she shouldn't have. Martha didn't mind in the least. "Oh, my dear, I most definitely am! I'm fifty!"

"Fifty!" Allie was genuinely shocked. Martha looked at least ten years younger.

Papouli sat forward and, with the excitement of a child playing a game, inquired, "How old do you think I am?"

Allie looked at him and gave a half laugh, sure that her first estimation of his age had to be way off base. She shook her head. "I don't know. When I first met you, I thought you were about sixty." Although she now knew that her other thought about him being ageless was probably closer to the truth. "You must be quite a bit older. Unless you adopted all your children."

"Ha!" Papouli laughed and, sitting back, slapped his hand against his skinny knee before proudly singing out, "I'm seventy-nine!"

"Papouli!" Allie loved the fact that he was a man who knew not to be afraid of the numbers going up on his biological clock, but rather to be proud and honored that he could live them. "Seventy-nine. What's in the water in this village that makes you all look so young, anyway?"

Proud as villagers are of their water, they all liked that, but Papouli, true to his calling, explained, "We do have very good spring water here in Kastro that reaches us from high in the mountains." He pointed in their majestic direction. "But that's not what keeps us young. It's having faith that God will direct our steps correctly each day, and it's having people—whether they be family members or friends—who love and care for us and like each of us for what and who we are."

Allie shook her head. "Then I don't think I'll look young for long." But at their crestfallen faces she quickly explained. "Oh, after much prayer, I'm quite certain that God wants me here," she qualified, remembering who she was talking to. "But except for you three and little Jeannie Andreas, nobody else seems to."

"Bah!" Papouli rocked back in his chair. "Give them time, Yatrinna. The people of Kastro really are good. They just have some things to work out, things that have nothing to do with you," he admonished.

"But they're so unfriendly. Is it because I'm a woman?" She really didn't believe that was the problem, but she hoped that her question might lead to some answers.

Papouli smiled, showing a mouth full of nearly perfect teeth between his beard and his mustache. "No, Yatrinna, your being a woman has nothing to do with it. In fact, the problem has nothing to do with you at all. It's something that goes back many years." He knitted his gray brows together and pulled thoughtfully on his pointed beard. "So far back that not even *I* can remember—"

"Papouli!" A young girl's happy shout interrupted him, and they all swiveled around to watch as Jeannie Andreas came bounding up the stairs holding a basket full of what looked to Allie like large leaves.

But when Allie's gaze landed on the man following the girl, her smile froze. And her heart pounded harder in her chest. But whether it was a warning beat or a glad one, she wasn't sure.

When Jeannie's father noticed her, he paused in his climb. It was an infinitesimal hesitation that held his right foot suspended for a moment longer than necessary over the step, telling as clearly as any words might that he wasn't happy about finding her on Papouli's veranda.

Not at all.

Allie saw that his face was just as grim as it had been when he'd discovered her in his spare apartment's bedroom earlier. Wryly, she wondered if she were sitting in his chair this time, in his place on Papouli's veranda. Goldilocks revisited, perhaps?

"Welcome, welcome." Martha hopped up from the edge of her seat and held out welcoming hands to the newcomers.

"They're figs! From our tree by the fountain," Jeannie informed all excitedly as she gave the basket to Martha. "Eva and I picked them and packed them in their leaves to protect them—just as you taught us, Papouli," she practically sang out, inadvertently explaining to Allie why it looked as though she carried a basket full of leaves.

"From the tree by the fountain? My favorite!" Papouli exclaimed, knowing how to please a child.

"I know." Jeannie beamed at being able to give the grandfatherly priest she adored something he loved. But when she noticed Allie sitting across the table, her eyes widened and she danced over to her side. "Yatrinna! I didn't know that you were here! I thought you were sleeping again."

Like a magnet drawn to iron, Allie's gaze was pulled to the girl's father. A muscle jumped in his jaw, and Allie knew he remembered finding her asleep in his house, too. The current that passed between them crackled.

Blushing, she shifted her eyes back to Jeannie. "No, one nap is all I get in a day, if I'm lucky." She hoped that the covering of night hid the tell-all signs of her red face.

"Ah..." Papouli commented prosaically, and Allie glanced sharply at him. From the twinkle that lit up his fine old eyes as he looked from her to the teacher, she knew that he had caught her blush—and worst of all, he knew the reason for it. What amazed Allie was how pleased he seemed by it. "You did get a chance to rest this afternoon, then?" his gravelly voice asked, and she was glad for his diplomacy.

She swallowed and nodded. "I fell asleep immediately—"

"And me and Baba found her sleeping on the bed just like Sleeping Beauty," Jeannie piped in. "And now she's going to live with us!"

"In the spare apartment," Stavros said quickly.

Papouli glanced above the rim of his glasses at the schoolteacher. "But where else would she live?"

Stavros looked sharply at the priest, as though Papouli had just told a joke that Stavros didn't find amusing.

"Sit—sit down and have fruit and coffee with us," Martha invited, and she and Natalia started to pull two more chairs up to the table.

"No, we won't stay," Stavros said, glancing at Allie.

"But Baba!" Jeannie cried.

Ignoring her, he turned to Natalia and said, "You must have

much to do to get ready for tomorrow. We just wanted to come and say good-bye and to wish you the very best." Jeannie opened her mouth again, and Stavros placed his hand on her shoulder and gently squeezed, quieting her. "You're leaving in the morning?"

Natalia nodded. "At 6:00 a.m."

That information seemed to distract Jeannie. "I don't want you to go," Jeannie whined, and leaving her father's side, she went over to Natalia and hugged her fiercely.

"I'll miss you, too, pumpkin." Natalia squeezed the girl close to her. "But at least you'll have the new doctor for company."

Jeannie stood back and looked over at Allie. A smile lit her face, replacing the sadness of before. "I know. And I'm sooo glad." She looked back at Natalia. "But you promise to come back...at least for visits?"

"I promise," Natalia said with the solemnity young children appreciate. "But you have to promise to come and visit me someday, too."

Jeannie's eyes widened. "Really?"

Natalia nodded. "Really."

Stavros reached for his daughter's hand. "Come on, pumpkin."

Reluctantly, Jeannie went with him. From the dejected slump of her shoulders, it was obvious to all she didn't want to go. But as she thought of something, joy, with the quickness of a light being flipped on, suddenly filled her features, and turning to Allie, she exclaimed, "I know! Why don't you come with us, Yatrinna? You don't know the path too well, and we live in the same house, after all." She laughed, the delighted laugh of a child who was thrilled with a situation.

But her father apparently wasn't. "Jeannie..." He directed

his words to his daughter, but his gaze swung over to Allie's as he sent her a strong nonverbal message not to accept the invitation. "Maybe Yatrinna wants to stay longer," he suggested pointedly.

Allie knew from the hard glint in his eye that he was warning her not to come with them.

And she bristled. If he had somehow asked her not to accept, she probably would have complied. But the warning was a challenge, and Allie rarely passed one up. Besides, wasn't he the one who had made her being a friend to Jeannie a condition to her living in the apartment?

And his daughter was right. It would be nice to walk the dark and unfamiliar path home with someone.

Toying with the strap of her purse, she answered Jeannie while looking at the man beside her. "Your father's right, Jeannie," she said. When she saw the look of relief that jumped into his eyes as he thought that she would decline the invitation, it almost kept her from her course.

Almost.

Not quite.

Using his own reasoning against him, she stood and continued, "I'm sure Natalia has much to do before leaving tomorrow. I should know after just moving, myself." His eyes flickered with something—guilt, anger? She wasn't sure which. But dropping her gaze to Jeannie's, she answered, "I would like very much to walk home with you."

"Hurray!" the girl shouted, but only the sound of coins being jiggled around in his pocket came from her father. Allie didn't look at him, but she could feel his glowering gaze on her, and for once, she wished she hadn't accepted a challenge. She knew that to back out now, though, would only worsen the situation and confuse Jeannie.

Turning to Natalia, she held out her hand. "I'm so glad we had the chance to meet."

"Me, too," Natalia agreed. "It would have been terrible had you arrived tomorrow and we missed each other. It really does make me feel good to know you are here to look after Martha and Baba."

Allie rolled her eyes. "I think it will be the other way around. They're going to be looking after me."

Natalia laughed her agreement. "They're good at that," she admitted.

"I hope you're happy in the city," Allie offered, and really meant it, even though she still couldn't imagine anyone wanting to trade Kastro for any metropolis, even Athens, which was one of her favorite places.

Natalia shrugged her graceful shoulders. "It's a great big, wonderful world out there. I'm looking forward to seeing it!"

That there was something very special about this young woman was obvious to Allie. Tilting her head speculatively to the side, she pronounced, "Natalia, I have a feeling that you're going to take it by storm."

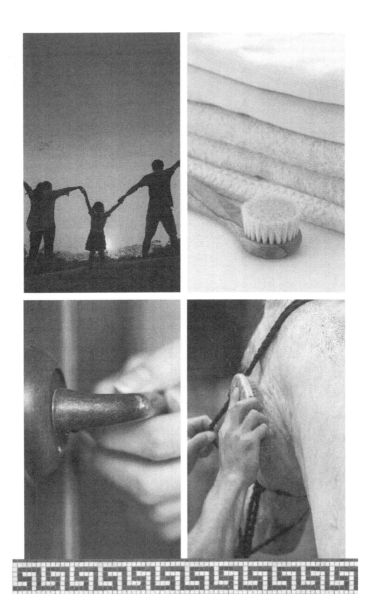

Chapter 7—A Soft Summer Night

The smooth, silky threads of night hung like an antique tapestry around the man, the woman, and the child.

It was just as Allie had always thought nightfall in the countryside would be. Their feet trod upon the sun-baked soil of the earth until they reached the cobbled steps that ran beside the Byzantine church. They then followed the stone walkway's meandering course up the mountainside toward their home.

With the setting of the sun, the cicadas had finally gone to sleep, the beam of the moon as it poked its face out from behind the ramparts of the castle being too cool to entice them to grind their legs in sound. But the summer song of the crickets now filled the warm air, along with the soft meow of two-month-old kittens and distant goat bells lightly flavoring the warm air with their tinkling notes.

It would have been perfect.

A glorious summer eve.

If. . .

The man walking on the other side of the little girl had been content.

But glancing over at Stavros Andreas, Allie knew he wasn't.

Not a bit.

And Allie knew it was because of her. She had come to his world, to his village, to his house, even, and had upset it. Allie could feel his unrest. It was palpable, hovering in the air around them, a discordant note, even as his daughter chattered on excitedly about her day.

Allie could see that his lips were a pale slash across his face and that his shoulders were held tensely at alert, like a man about to have an unpleasant medical procedure performed on him. Their afternoon conversation might have ended with his agreement to let her rent his apartment, but Allie was sure that the progressing hours of the day had only brought unease over that decision.

From the first, he hadn't wanted her in his house.

He still didn't.

She didn't have to be a mind reader to know that if he could come up with a way to get rid of her without upsetting his daughter, he would. But that was something Allie couldn't let happen. She needed to live in his spare apartment. Other than the fact that there was nowhere else in the village suitable for her, the house already felt like home. She depended on its friendly walls to return to every day.

Again, she regretted challenging him at Papouli's house. She knew that he hadn't wanted her to accompany them now. What she didn't know was what had made her push him.

Perhaps the warmth and friendship from the priest's house, combined with her romantic nature, signaled for something more with the teacher and had made her professional mantle slip.

It was a mistake she wouldn't make again.

She couldn't let herself forget that her professional standing and his daughter's needs were the only reasons he had finally relented and agreed to let her live in the apartment. To try for friendship or to contest his desires concerning their tenuous landlord-tenant new relationship might provoke a problem. Remembering her lack of welcome in this village that afternoon, Allie knew that she had enough issues to deal with as it was.

From now on, she would treat him politely but formally.

Nothing else.

She was Kastro's doctor.

A relationship with a man in such a small village would set her up for ethical problems again.

A relationship with her landlord would spell disaster. She wouldn't let her physician's persona slip again. She would be cool and professional.

She looked down at the little girl who chattered on about her escapades in picking figs, and she smiled.

And she would be Jeannie's good friend.

***

What most upset Stavros was not the fact that he had to share his house with her, but rather, with her coming, he had learned just how badly his daughter missed having a mother. Up to that inauspicious moment when Jeannie had begged him to let the doctor live in the other apartment, Stavros had convinced himself that he had succeeded in being both father and mother to her. He had, in fact, prided himself on thinking that he had filled both roles as well as any two parents ever could.

But looking at his daughter as she talked animatedly to the doctor, a different lilting sound to her voice from that which she normally had, he now knew differently.

And it bothered him.

A lot.

He didn't want to involve anybody else in their lives. As long as he and Jeannie were self-sufficient, he felt secure. Pain could be avoided; it could be prevented.

He knew very well that having Allie Alexander living in the apartment next door would spell involvement. It was inevitable.

His fingers jingled the coins sitting in his pocket.

With her living anywhere in the village, it would happen.

In spite of what he might want, even in spite of what she might want, this attraction between them was too strong.

He glanced over Jeannie's head toward the woman. Her head was tilted to the side and slightly lowered, an elegant braid falling over her right shoulder as she paid attention to what Jeannie had to say as if it was the most important thing in the world.

When her gaze suddenly lifted and touched upon his, it happened again.

That spark. That fusion.

But this time there was something different. A cover seemed to slide over the quicksilver in her eyes as a cool, professional quality came into them. It made him feel as though he had just been shut out on a cold winter's day.

He frowned.

She didn't challenge him but simply dropped her gaze back to Jeannie as if he was of no more concern to her than a distant relative of a patient.

But Stavros had been a man long enough to know when a woman was attracted to him. She might have him believe that she couldn't care less about what was between them. But he knew she did. She cared.

But like him, she didn't seem to want to do anything about it.

It made his mind glad.

But not his heart, which had remained dormant until he had seen her, talked to her. Now it was beating in want of more out of life. His heart had nearly broken when he didn't find that right relationship with Jeannie's mother.

He moved the coins in his pocket around with more force.

No. He didn't want a relationship.

He didn't want involvement with any woman. It would be unwise to mess with the stability he had created in his life, in Jeannie's life.

Jeannie's laughter rang out, and it occurred to Stavros that maybe having Jeannie around could protect the doctor and himself from an entanglement neither he nor she seemed to want. It might not be all that difficult with his daughter to run buffer for them.

That was his bright idea until…

His daughter suddenly turned traitor. Taking a hold of first his hand then the doctor's, it was as if they were all connected somehow. It was suddenly too familiar, too—

"It's like we're a family!" Jeannie sang out, clutching each adult hand proudly out in front of her.

And Stavros knew that was it.

It *was* like they were a family.

A nice normal family.

And he learned then that having a child around was not a cushion against involvement. Jeannie would not make a good chaperone at all.

"We even live in the same house!" Jeannie continued blithely along, and Stavros would have liked to have taken masking tape and taped his daughter's cute, little, big mouth shut.

The doctor's gaze shot over to his, and Stavros was sure he saw amusement in the silver bits of light that danced in their cool depths.

He was surprised when she opened her mouth to answer Jeannie, but relieved, too. It was nice not to have to be the one to think up a response to an embarrassing statement made by his child.

"We might be in the same house, Jeannie"—her soft voice was tuned toward Jeannie, but Stavros could have sworn that she was actually talking to him—"but we're in different apartments. So it's like we're in an apartment building."

"Except for the bathroom," Jeannie pointed out, as if that made all the difference.

"Except for the bathroom," Allie agreed, and Stavros was certain he hadn't imagined the resigned note in her voice. He suspected then that she wasn't as easy with the sharing of the house's only bathroom as she had earlier let on. The thought somehow pleased him.

"Oh!" Jeannie sang out as she remembered something. Letting go of their hands, she skipped ahead of them and walked backward, facing them both. "I've come up with the perfect signal so we know when the bathroom is in use."

Allie's gaze bounced over to Stavros.

He saw it coming his way, but he didn't catch it.

He let her gaze rebound off him and looked away.

Knowing from now on exactly when she was using the bathroom—the bathtub, in particular—didn't seem like a very good solution to him.

"I drew a sign on a piece of cardboard that says IN USE and put it on the hall table," Jeannie went on, the innocence of childhood hiding from her the undercurrent of tension that ran between the adults. "It fits perfectly under both of our doors."

"Great, pumpkin," Stavros mumbled, but all he could really think about was the next year. He could plainly see his future, sitting on the sofa correcting test papers and having the sign pushed under the hall door. It would be a viable reminder of the beautiful woman who was a part of his world, while not being a part of it.

It was going to drive him crazy. It already was. Knowing she was so close and yet not in the way he wanted her to be…

He decided that he would have to start correcting all tests at school.

But what about when he was making supper, helping Jeannie with her homework, or writing on the computer? He couldn't leave his own house. Maybe he would spend more time down in the stable with Charger.

"What a smart girl you are." Stavros heard Allie commend Jeannie, but from the way she stumbled over her words, he was absolutely certain that she was uncomfortable with the whole idea. It softened his own trepidation and, in a crooked sort of way, satisfied him.

"Thank you." Jeannie gave a little bow and beamed up at the grown-ups, blessedly oblivious to the feelings that swarmed around them like hornets ready to bite.

And about half an hour later, Allie wished that she had been as smart as Jeannie when, after a soak in the elegant bathtub, one that had her feeling like visiting royalty, she opened the bathroom door just in time to see Stavros—in the central hall— pushing the IN USE sign under her apartment door.

Realizing too late that she had forgotten to put the signal under his door when she went in for her bath, and wanting only to disappear, she took a sudden and very guilty step back into the bathroom. She might have made it unnoticed if her flip-flop hadn't met with a puddle of bathwater, which had effectively transformed the floor into a skating rink and her into a moving mass on a bull's-eye course for Stavros's broad back.

"Oh no!" she yelled out a split second before she slammed into him.

"What the—?" he grunted and swung around to face her, his hands automatically reaching out to steady her.

"I'm sorry," Allie gasped, her fingers clutching his shirt sleeves as she re-gained her balance.

She was panting.

He was holding her close.

Their eyes met.

She felt Stavros draw in his breath before disgust exploded from him. "Don't you know that wet marble and flip-flops are a lethal combination?" he croaked out.

"Yes, I…" She looked down at the floor and kicked off the offending shoes, knowing that it was much safer to walk barefoot on wet marble than to wear rubber footwear. "I wasn't thinking."

"Obviously," he ground out and swung his eyes to the sign, which he had just planted partway under her door. "What happened to the IN USE signal?"

His tone made Allie feel like a teenager caught sneaking into her bedroom after curfew. She didn't like it, and a quick retort rose in her throat. But in fairness, she knew she should have remembered the sign. In the name of their tenuous landlord-tenant relationship, she swallowed her sharp words and let a simple apology come out instead. "I'm sorry. I forgot."

"Since we have agreed to use the sign, at least don't forget to use it."

Clutching her dressing gown tighter against her, she said, "It won't happen again."

"Make sure that it doesn't," he commanded, and his tone chafed against Allie's mind like sandpaper against her skin, and a quick retort wouldn't be held down this time. "Look, I said I was sorry. But couldn't you hear the water running?" That seemed logical enough to Allie. Water running through pipes was not soundproof, and, too, there was the noise of the water pump.

"If I had been in my apartment, I would have. But I was with Charger."

She blinked. "Charger?"

"My horse," he explained.

"Oh." She remembered his horse—the white horse. The horse he had been riding when she had thought he was a prince in a fairy tale…

A heavy settling sigh, like the last blast in a windstorm, rumbled from his chest, reminding Allie of how much had changed since that first meeting. "Look," he said, running his hand distractedly through his already tousled hair. Only his cowlick—a permanent rumple—remained in place. "I would appreciate it if you would try not to forget to put the sign out," he said, a definite request this time, with a vulnerable quality to his voice that reminded Allie of a patient in pain, begging for whatever relief she might have to give. It was something she knew how to respond to.

"I won't forget." Her voice was soft, much softer than she had intended it to be, and confused by her own reaction, she lowered her lids and brushed past him to push open the door to her apartment.

But as Allie slowly backed in, once again their gazes found one another, and Allie saw what this encounter was costing him. He had the look of a man who was confused about what he wanted, what he needed. His features were tainted with a grim sadness that was one of the most vulnerable looks she had ever seen. As her door clicked shut, she wondered what dreams and hopes had to have died in his life to have colored his face with such a naked and world-weary pain.

And she knew then that her first impression of him had been correct: He was a prince of a man, one who was definitely hurting, one who had things to overcome, but a prince nonetheless.

And one whom Allie liked. A lot.

An hour later she reclined in bed, gazing in the soft moon glow at the picture of Dale that she had placed on her bedside table. Dale's blond hair and laughing blue eyes slowly seemed to fade away as her eyes drifted shut, to be replaced by those of a man with dark brown hair and even darker eyes. Troubled eyes, they seemed to be asking something of her.

But what? She wasn't sure.

It was, however, something Allie was determined to discover.

And soon.

Chapter 8—Helping Hands

A rooster crowed, a horse neighed, and Allie reveled in the feeling of the sun as its morning-time fingers of welcome gently washed her face.

She stretched out across the comfortable bed and smiled, a slow smile of contentment and peace.

Not a motor could be heard running, nor a horn blowing, nor even a garbage truck moaning. The sounds that surrounded her were all a part of the wonderful world of nature, real and balanced.

With exuberance for the new day, she hopped out of bed, and reaching for her dressing gown, she padded on bare feet across the wooden floor to the window.

Throwing the French doors wide, she stepped out onto the sunlit balcony and breathed in the fresh, pine-scented mountain air. She knew the heat wave had no intentions of abating for several more days. By the afternoon it would be another scorcher in a long line of them. So she relished the night-cooled air that tenaciously clung to the mountainside. The famous Hellenic haze, suffusing the landscape and making it look like an impressionist painting of the purest school, already covered the valley. But it hadn't reached the mountain heights yet, and it wouldn't until noon. Not even the cicadas had started grinding their legs yet, something they had been doing at least two hours earlier the day before in Athens.

The regal steps of a horse prancing below her balcony drew her gaze downward. Her breath caught at the sight of the schoolteacher sitting tall and elegant upon the same white stallion she had seen him astride the previous day.

The horse was arrogant and impressive.

So was the man.

As if sensing her gaze on him, the man looked up, and for a split moment, it was as the previous day when they had been strangers traveling in opposite directions. There was interest and wonder and romance in his deep-set eyes, not even a hint of the vulnerable man Allie had caught sight of the night before. That man was well hidden behind this man's solidly composed features, and the one before her now was once again a storybook prince wearing assurance that everything would turn out perfectly in his land. It had to. Nobody would want to read about his exploits if it didn't.

Allie shook her head.

It wasn't the previous day.

And they were no longer strangers.

They were real people who had to deal with the real world and real emotions. She knew now, as he slightly inclined his head toward her in greeting and clip-clopped off, that he was much more than a storybook prince. He was a man who was trying the best he knew how to handle the situations that life had thrown at him. She breathed out an automatic prayer for him while watching his straight back disappear down the lane. She wondered just what those circumstances had been—in particular, how it was that his daughter was motherless.

But with an office to get in order, Allie knew that she couldn't let anything or any emotions get in the way of what she had come to Kastro to do. Stepping back into her room, she drew the cream-colored curtains together, and then pushing all thoughts of her handsome landlord to a far corner of her brain, she went to the central hall, shoved the IN USE sign under the schoolteacher's door, and was happy to use the bathroom knowing that the apartment next door was currently empty of its male occupant. Back in her bedroom alcove, she donned a pair of jeans and a T-shirt. Then she padded over to the kitchen area and put as many cleaning supplies as she found under the sink into a plastic pail, and taking her medical bag—just in case of an emergency—she left her home and started the short walk down the narrow, cobbled street to her office. Since the good people of Kastro didn't seem to care that the clinic was in shambles, she knew that it was up to her to clean it and ready it for use.

She met several of Kastro's citizens along the way. Half of them totally ignored her, while the other half smiled shyly, mumbled a good-morning, and quickly went on their way. But Allie's knowing eyes didn't miss how they all looked over their shoulders, as if to check out who might be watching them speak to her.

She shook her head minutely after each such encounter and continued down the cobbled lane. A few minutes later, she stepped into the courtyard of the clinic, greeted the friendly tortoise of the day before, and swung open the office door. Casting her gaze around its dismal interior, she sighed. It needed even more work than she had remembered.

Not wasting time thinking about it, she opened all the windows and shutters—but not the back door where she supposed the donkey still to be—then, taking a pair of surgical gloves from her bag, she collected all the trash that had been left around the rooms. That completed, she was standing in the examining room contemplating tackling the medicine cabinet—and the scorpion within—when she heard laughter coming from the waiting room.

"Allie...?" Martha's friendly voice called out, and Allie's

soul rejoiced at the warmhearted greeting.

"In here," she sang out and turned gladly away from the grimy doors of the cabinet. But it wasn't Martha who came bounding into the examining room, it was Jeannie.

"Hi, Yatrinna!"

"Jeannie!" Allie exclaimed and smiled over at Martha as she trailed behind the bubbly girl. "How wonderful to see you. But"—she motioned down to the cleaning supplies each held and shook her head in question—"what's this?"

Holding a feather duster up in front of her, Jeannie shouted out their reason for coming. "We've come to help clean the office!"

"What?" Allie looked from the child to the adult. "How did you know that was what I was doing?"

"I saw you leave the house with that stuff." Jeannie pointed over to where Allie's cleaning things sat in a corner. "And I told Miss Martha."

"A good thing you did, too." Martha commended Jeannie while casting her gaze quickly and thoroughly around the room. "I knew that it was in need of some cleaning, but this"—she made a disgusted sound—"this is terrible." She turned to Allie. "It's not fitting that you should have to clean the office at all, much less alone."

"I don't mind," Allie murmured, but she was touched by Martha's concern.

"Well, I do," Martha spoke firmly. "Anybody in this village is capable of cleaning, but not one other person can do the job you've been hired to do."

"Martha, thanks, but"—Allie shrugged her shoulders—"it's not your problem."

"The bad behavior of my neighbors," Martha said as she

pulled a brightly colored kerchief out of her skirt pocket and tied it over her hair, "is most definitely my problem." But seeing that Allie felt uncomfortable with her cleaning, Martha paused and gave another reason, one that was just as truthful. A gentle, hurting softness touched the older woman's voice. "Besides, I promised Natalia that I would look after you. She knows that I….need to keep busy."

For all of Martha's assurances of the night before, Allie knew that Martha was in pain over her sister's leaving. She missed Natalia, pure and simple, just as people the world over miss loved ones who have to go out and make their way in life.

"Did she get off all right this morning?" Allie asked quietly.

Martha nodded. "She was as excited and as high-strung as a thoroughbred ready to run the race of her life." She paused and sighed. "But she was ready."

Allie's smile deepened. "She'll be fine."

"I know, but I do miss her. Please let me help you. I need to do something," she admitted on a near desperate whisper.

Allie pursed her lips and remembered how she'd felt when her brother, Alex, had left home for good. It had felt like the ending of a good book she had borrowed from the library, meaning that she couldn't even take it off the shelf and read it again whenever she wanted. Nodding, she admitted, "I would be very grateful for your help."

"I miss Natalia, too!" Jeannie sang out. "I want to help, too."

Allie and Martha turned to the girl and laughed. "You may!" Allie flicked the girl's ponytail. She grimaced toward the cabinet. "But please be careful. I saw a scorpion run up its side yesterday."

By way of answer, Martha leaned over and, pulling a can of bug spray from her pail, loudly proclaimed, "Lead the way. I'm an expert on getting rid of scorpions."

Jeannie giggled. "She's not a ghostbuster—she's a bugbuster! You should have seen the scorpions that were living in our house when Daddy and I first moved in for good."

Allie looked sharply at Jeannie. "In your house…?" she echoed. Jeannie's house meant her house. Had she slept where scorpions slept? Allie hugged herself and rubbed her hands up and down her goose-bumped arms.

Jeannie giggled again and took a hold of Allie's hand. "Don't worry, Yatrinna. We don't have them anymore."

"That's right," Martha quickly piped in and, holding the can of spray up like a banner, proclaimed, "I annihilated them!"

The three worked diligently, and by two o'clock, when it was much too warm to work any longer, they had accomplished what Allie was sure would have taken her at least two days had she been alone.

Martha was out finding a new home for the donkey, and Jeannie was out getting rid of the trash, while Allie mopped the floor for the final time. She had been amazed to discover that under all the grime was a beautiful marble floor of golden white. Finished, she was smiling over the transformation cleaning had wrought to the two rooms when the shadow of a very large man fell across the still-wet section in front of her.

A bit surprised that someone would walk in without calling out a greeting, Allie nonetheless turned with a welcoming smile on her lips. But when she saw who it was, the mop slipped out of her hand and crashed with a loud clatter onto the hard floor.

The ogre stood before her, and his expression wasn't any friendlier than it had been the previous day. Even worse, he was looking around the office as if he were the proprietor.

"May I help you?" Allie asked politely, but the fingers of

apprehension that crawled across her sweat-dampened back alerted her to the fact that his visit was not going to be a friendly one.

He stared down at her, the line of his mouth becoming long and thin before his whiny voice sounded out between it. "No. I just came by to see what you were doing."

That, Allie thought, was obvious. What was equally apparent was that he was up to no good. She was about to say something scathing when Martha walked in from the backyard.

"I took the donkey to the field behind the church…Tasos." She paused when she saw him and greeted him with a familiar smile. "How nice to see you."

Nice? *Nice* was not a word Allie would have used to describe the man's visit.

"What are you doing here, Martha?" the man called Tasos, but the one Allie still thought of as the ogre, snapped out. For the first time, Allie realized that Martha might have stepped over a line, a picket line of sorts, in coming to help her. It concerned her.

But it shouldn't have.

Martha was a woman of faith whom no one could browbeat. Plus, being the priest's daughter put her in a neutral position in village politics, something she was about to show Allie she knew how to use wisely.

"I'm doing what every other man, woman, and child in this village should be doing. Cleaning this disreputable clinic." She turned to Allie and asked, "Have you met?" But not waiting for a reply, she quickly introduced them. "Dr. Allie Alexander, this is Tasos Drakopoulos."

Allie's lips quirked at the mention of the man's name, and she thought that if she had known it before, she would have dubbed him "Dracula" rather than "ogre."

True to her quick way of talking and moving, Martha admonished, "Honestly, Tasos, you were in charge of this clinic—"

Allie looked sharply over at the man. He was in charge of the clinic? So he had known precisely the condition in which she had found it the previous day.

"How could you let the new doctor come into such a dirty, unsightly place?" Martha continued voicing Allie's very question, but with a tone that Allie was sure she had probably used when they had been children growing up together and Tasos had tormented a cat or a dog. "It's embarrassing to the good name of our village," Martha finished.

But Martha was wasting her breath. Tasos Drakopoulos showed no remorse. Motioning with his thick thumb toward the boxes that Allie had discovered contained equipment far in excess to that which was normally supplied to rural doctors' offices—an EKG machine, a miniature ICU case, and all the equipment needed to perform emergency surgery—he snorted out, "I got all those things brought here, didn't I?" And not waiting for or wanting a reply, he turned on his big feet and stomped off through the door.

Allie turned to Martha. "He had all these supplies brought here? Yet he has obviously been the one to turn many villagers against me."

Moving quickly around the room, Martha gathered cleaning supplies while answering. "As my father told you last night, it's their problem, not yours. When the people of Kastro need a doctor, they'll come to you." For all Martha's talking— and while they had been working, she proved just how much and how fast she talked—Allie had quickly come to learn that

Martha took the admonishments about the taming of the tongue, found in the third chapter of James, seriously. She would never gossip about her neighbors. It was a trait Allie couldn't help but admire in the other woman.

"I hope so," Allie murmured, but she wasn't so sure any longer. Something deep and ugly was going on in Kastro, and she didn't like not knowing what it was.

Martha paused in her work and touched Allie's arm in a comforting way before motioning to the spotless room. "I think we've done very well. This evening we'll whitewash it."

Jeannie rushed into the office and, hearing the last of Martha words, shouted out, "Me, too! I love whitewashing!"

"You, too!" Martha agreed. "You've been a big help. But for now," Martha spoke as she rinsed off her hands in the now sparkling sink, "it's lunchtime and siesta time." She looked at Allie. "My father asked that you come and eat with us."

"No!" Jeannie interjected, causing the two women to look at her in surprise. "Come eat with Baba and me! I know Baba would like for you to come. All the doctors have practically lived at our house!" Looking at her, Allie was sure that the girl spoke the truth about the other doctors. But she was also sure that such an invitation wouldn't apply to her.

"Thank you, Jeannie." She looked over at Martha and smiled. "Thank you both. But I think I'd like to go and pick up a few things from the store and just go back to my apartment, eat something light, and take a little rest." At the fallen look that crossed Jeannie's face, Allie quickly went on, "But you and I can walk down here together this evening. All right?"

Allie was glad to see that the suggestion brought the shine back to Jeannie's eyes. "All right."

They closed up the office that now smelled of disinfectant

and bug spray, and after Martha directed Allie to one of the shops in the village that was just up the road from the clinic, the three split up, promising to meet again that evening.

Chapter 9 — The Village Store

Allie found the store. And she was impressed.

It was located on the bottom floor of a home that was of the same period as the schoolteacher's. When she pushed aside the beads that admitted air, not flies, Allie felt as though she had stepped through a portal in time.

It could have been a mercantile shop of a hundred years earlier, with lovingly arranged displays set attractively on shelves made of the finest mahogany. A large antique counter, with flowers carved into its rich wood, was the focal point of the room. Allie walked over to it and lightly tapped her fingers against the shining silver bell that sat next to a masterfully gilded cash register.

She had to wait only a moment before a very pregnant older woman emerged from behind the curtain. She looked like a Victorian mother, and Allie was sure that the child she was carrying had to be the latest of many.

"Oh," the woman exclaimed in a voice that was hardly louder than a whisper, while she self-consciously glanced over her shoulder toward the curtained-off area of the shop. Allie wanted to feel irritated by the gesture, one she had experienced too many times that morning while walking to the clinic. But she wasn't, especially when the woman readily extended her one hand in welcome while resting the other protectively against her protruding tummy. "You must be the new doctor."

Allie took the woman's small hand in her own and wondered at the nervous way she again looked behind her. That someone in the back room probably held the views of the ogre, of Tasos Drakopoulos, was obvious. But the sparkle in the woman's eyes made it equally apparent that she did not.

Allie nodded, then said, "I'm Allie Alexander."

"Welcome to Kastro, Yatrinna." Allie was pleasantly surprised by the proprietress's use of her title. Even more so when the woman whispered her own name. "I'm Sophia Drakopoulos."

Allie's fingers let go of the woman's hand as if it had suddenly turned into a scorpion. Could this sweet woman possibly be the ogre's wife? "Are you by any chance related to Tasos Drakopoulos?" Allie found herself asking.

The light left the woman's eyes as, with a quick glance over her shoulder, she whispered, "By marriage I am."

"Oh." Allie didn't know what else to say. How could she tell the woman that she couldn't stand her ogre of a husband? But more than anything, Allie was amazed that Martha had instructed her to come to this shop. Martha had to have understood how she felt about Tasos Drakopoulos.

Allie's gaze fell to the woman's tummy.

Tasos Drakopoulos's baby?

It seemed an ironic twist that her first patient would probably be the wife of the person she least liked in the village. "When is your baby due?" Allie finally asked, her professionalism holding her in good stead.

"Soon," the woman answered, and Allie's trained ears heard a wistfulness behind the word.

"How many children do you have?"

The woman's shoulders sagged, and she looked—with what Allie could only describe as hope—down at her growing child. "This baby…she's all I have."

Allie was troubled by the woman's reply. The doctor in her

wanted to ask several questions. But she knew that now was neither the time nor the place. "I should have the clinic opened by tomorrow evening. Please come, and we'll talk." Tasos Drakopoulos's family or not, Allie worked according to the Hippocratic Oath. Besides, in spite of the man this woman was married to, Allie knew that she liked Sophia Drakopoulos. Even after a few moments, Allie recognized the woman as one of the world's human "angels."

With joy lines painting her face—one that reminded Allie of a porcelain doll she used to have—Sophia looked up from the baby, whose face she had yet to see, to Allie's, and she spoke in a voice that Allie thought might have belonged to a mouse, if one could talk. "When I found out that the new doctor was a woman...well"—she lowered her shy eyes again—"I was very glad, and I thought...that maybe...*maybe*...this baby might be born safely...since you're here."

Allie was certain now that the woman had had trouble having children. Her medical curiosity wouldn't be held down any longer. "Mrs. Drakopoulos—"

"Sophia." She stopped Allie with a hesitant smile. "Please," she quietly suggested, "call me Sophia."

"Sophia." Allie smiled her thanks before continuing. "You have had other pregnancies?"

Sophia nodded, and Allie didn't miss the tears that highlighted her eyes. "Several. My husband and I have wanted a child for many years but—" At the sound of the beads in the doorway being shoved impatiently aside, Sophia clamped down on her words, and Allie could feel tension radiating from her as she looked at the woman who had just barged into the shop. Nodding toward the newcomer, Sophia softly said, "I'll be right with you, Elani."

Curious, Allie turned to the woman, but when she saw a replica of the sour-faced, Dionysia from the *kafenion*, Allie wished that she had checked her interest. The venom that radiated from this woman, though, made Dionysia, in comparison, seem like a saint. Her eyes held a fever, a fever of hate, while her lips held all the cold of an arctic winter. No smile lines marked her middle-aged face; rather, lines of discontent and enmity radiated from her lips like ill-placed spider webs.

Nodding, Allie turned back to Sophia and, as was the custom in villages, she handed the proprietress her shopping list. As Sophia gathered the things from the various shelves, Allie would have gladly ignored the other customer if the woman's hard voice hadn't broken the heavy silence with the force of a sledgehammer against stone.

"So, you must be the new doctor," she crackled out, and as Allie turned to face her again, she couldn't help but be reminded of the wicked witch in *The Wizard of Oz*. This woman would not have needed makeup to play the role, nor even to modify her voice. She was positively perfect for the part.

Allie nodded. "And you are—?"

The small woman's lips pursed together, showing how the sour lines had been etched into her face, as she boastfully replied, "Elani Drakopoulos, wife of Tasos Drakopoulos, the mayor of this village."

Allie's gaze flew over to Sophia, and relief coursed through her as she realized that she had been mistaken in assuming that "being related by marriage" meant that Sophia was married to Tasos Drakopoulos. Sophia was too nice to be married to the ogre.

Allie looked back at the woman with the pointy chin. This woman, on the other hand, was the perfect match for him. "Well,

Kyria Drakopoulos, the clinic should be open by tomorrow evening." Allie wasn't going to waste the opportunity to let Drakopoulos know that she was in charge of her job, regardless of his attempts to dissuade her. "Please let your friends—and family—know."

The woman's sharp face rose higher still, as if she were a cat sniffing the air. "If I or my family"—she looked toward Sophia, and Allie could tell that she was sending her kinsman a strong hint—"should require the services of a physician, then we shall send for a cab and have it take us down to the city so that we may visit a specialist," she proclaimed, and turning her back on Allie, she demanded of Sophia, "Do hurry, Sophia. I'm a busy woman, and I haven't got all day."

With a soft grace Allie was coming to expect from her, Sophia gave a slight nod toward Elani but continued to gather Allie's supplies without being harried or bothered by her relative.

Allie decided she wouldn't be, either. She refrained from telling Kyria Drakopoulos that she was herself a specialist, specializing in family medicine, and instead watched as Sophia put her purchases into two bags. She paid for them. But when she noticed some things in the bags that she hadn't written on her list and for which she was sure she hadn't paid, she was about to point them out to Sophia when her new friend subtly shook her head, warning her not to say anything. With her sweet smile, she gently placed her hand over Allie's and mouthed the words, "Welcome, Yatrinna."

Allie understood that Sophia was welcoming her with gifts of homemade rose-petal jam, fresh-picked oregano, and mountain tea. Smiling her thanks, Allie pushed the beads aside and walked out into the heat of the day. She didn't even mind that Elani Drakopoulos had prudishly turned her back on her again. Sophia's kindness had more than made up for the other woman's pettiness, and best of all, Allie knew that in Sophia, she had another friend in Kastro.

***

"Baba," Jeannie questioned her father when he sat down at the table across from her, "may I say grace?"

Stavros looked sharply at her. He knew that something important was going on in her little head. Normally he had to encourage her to say grace. Not having a mother to confide in, she had fallen into the habit of using grace as a means of telling him about things that were important to her little girl's heart but she was too shy to come right out and say.

Smiling, he nodded his head, glad that she had found this outlet. He wanted her to always feel as though she could tell him what was on her mind, even if she felt it necessary to tell God at the same time.

Looking like the classic picture of a child praying, Jeannie very primly and solemnly clasped her hands together and, lowering her head, ran through her normal prayer. "Thank You, God, for this food, for rest and home and all things good. For wind and rain, and sun above, but most of all for those we love!"

Stavros waited with his own head bowed. He knew that grace wasn't over until she said "Amen." Finally, with added warmth to her words, she continued, "And God…thank You for bringing Yatrinna to our house." She took a deep breath before sighing out, "She's one of those…I love."

Stavros's gazed lifted again to the bent head of his daughter. He knew she liked the new doctor, but loved?

"And, God," Jeannie continued to speak, totally confident that God was listening, "please help Daddy to like her more… and…to trust You more, too." Startled and convicted, Stavros widened his eyes until the little girl closed her prayer with "Amen." He quickly lowered his head again, not wanting her to catch him looking at her.

When he finally raised it, Jeannie was eating her French fries and fish sticks. She wore the trust that only children seem able to don comfortably. She believed totally that her prayer had been heard and would be answered in exactly the right way. She didn't have to concern herself with it any longer. Stavros wished he had a portion of that trust. He knew that he had had such a trust and faith…once upon a time… Even in his adult life. But that had been long, long ago.

He watched her for a moment before reaching for his own fork. He had to clarify a few things. "Jeannie, I don't dislike the new doctor," he said carefully.

"But you don't like her as much as you liked the other doctors," Jeannie pointed out and dipped a fry into ketchup.

"I like her," he said, defending himself. "Just…in a different way." *A very different way.*

"Then why haven't you invited her over to eat with us or to watch TV or anything?" she protested.

The *anything* was the problem. The *anything* was what worried him, and what, he suspected, worried the doctor, too. But he couldn't tell his daughter that. "Well…" He fished around for a reason, any reason but the real one. "Don't forget, she just came yesterday."

Jeannie's face brightened. "Then we can invite her to eat dinner with us tonight!"

Stavros felt his lips quirk. His daughter could deliberate a cause just like—his blood ran cold as he realized what he was thinking. That his daughter could deliberate a cause just like—a lawyer. Just like her mother could.

"Can we, Baba?"

Stavros shook himself and looked deeply into his daughter's imploring eyes, eyes that were the mirror of his own in a face that was the female version of his. But that didn't mean Jeannie hadn't inherited something from her mother. His jaw tensed as he admitted to himself that she might have her mother's ability to reason through an argument, but he would make good and sure that she would use her ability correctly, not just for her own professional glory and monetary attainment.

"Can we, Baba?" Jeannie prompted again, bringing him back to the problem at hand. Two other things he had learned from Jeannie's prayer were that he had to start acting more normally toward the doctor—and toward God.

He knew his faith had been severely weakened by his wife's desertion of them—he just hadn't realized until that moment that Jeannie had realized it, too. He had always taken her to church on Sundays and other holy days such as Christmas and Easter and had taught her how to say her prayers. It had never even occurred to him that his daughter had noticed his own lack.

He had prayed so hard that his wife would decide she wanted their child with whom she had "mistakenly" become pregnant. Somehow, Stavros had kept her from doing the unthinkable... A shudder passed through him. He couldn't even think about that frightening time, when his unborn baby's life could have legally been cut short. He still broke into a cold sweat thinking about it.

But his wife had never wanted the baby, never wanted Jeannie. Stavros had thought that when she saw the little life they had made together, she would change. He had prayed so hard for it to be so. But his wife never even held Jeannie. Not once. She had only wanted her career.

What good had all his praying, all his imploring to God done? Nothing. Not only had his wife deserted their baby and him years earlier, but then, six months ago, she had had to go and die, too. While on a business trip, of course.

"Ba...ba..." Jeannie impatiently called out and put her fork down on her plate with a loud clatter, effectively cutting into his reflections. He looked at her—the most dear being in the world to him—and knew she would refuse to eat another bite until he answered her.

"Yes, pumpkin." He came to a sudden decision—at least about the physician—one that made him feel good in a way he hadn't felt in a very long time. "I think it would be very nice to invite the doctor to dinner. We'll see if she's free tonight."

"Yippee!" Jeannie exclaimed, and picking up her fork, she stabbed a carrot. All was right in her world again.

There was a moment of thoughtful silence before Stavros spoke again. "I'm very proud of you for helping out at the clinic today."

His daughter beamed up at him, and while dipping a piece of bread into the olive oil dressing Stavros had poured over the tomato salad, she said, "We killed three scorpions, too!"

It was obvious to him that Jeannie thought that was the best part of the cleaning expedition. But it wasn't to Stavros. A frown, a father's instinct to be concerned for his child, sliced across his face. "Be careful," he admonished. "Their sting can really hurt."

"Don't worry. Yatrinna has medicine for bug bites, and if I got stung—" She stopped speaking at the sound of someone's light footsteps coming up the stairs. Leaning toward her father, she whispered, "That's Yatrinna." As the sound of the steps passed the door, Jeannie swiveled around in her chair to watch as the doctor passed by the open window.

When Jeannie waved to her, Allie waved back.

Stavros watched his daughter. She was so happy about the new doctor being a woman. But at that moment Stavros knew that it wasn't just that Allie was a woman. Rather, it was the woman Allie Alexander was. She had affected both Jeannie and him with her way of being.

Allie was good for Jeannie—very good. And anyone who was good for Jeannie made him glad.

Plus, the talk about scorpions had him admitting to himself that he liked having a doctor in the house again, even if the doctor was a woman who made him feel things he didn't want to feel.

"I like her," Jeannie said as she continued to watch the window where Allie had just passed. "She's so pretty and nice and—"

"Eek—" A bloodcurdling scream rent the air. A scream that both Stavros and Jeannie knew had come from the subject of their discussion. The doctor.

Chapter 10—Feud

"Stay put!" Stavros ordered his frightened daughter, and in a flash he was out the door and running toward the now silent doctor. In that split instant of time before he turned the corner of the veranda, he would have preferred to have still heard her screaming. With the quiet, he didn't know what he would find, and fear, like a searing blade, sliced through him.

He found her leaning against the railing, motionless, her hands covering her eyes. Dread moved in to keep the fear within him company. Had something happened to her eyes, those beautiful eyes that could darken like velvet and yet flash like quicksilver?

"Allie!" Her given name rolled naturally from his lips, and when her hands left her face and he saw that she was physically uninjured, his knees almost buckled with relief. But the haunted look that glazed her normally clear expression told of another type of injury, one that was perhaps just as scary. "Allie." He pulled her into his arms. She was trembling. "What is it?" he demanded, concern making his voice gruff.

Allie motioned, but didn't look, toward her front door.

Stavros turned to it, grimaced at what he saw, then pulled the woman named Allie Alexander closer to him. He wanted somehow to shield her, to protect her, from a situation that was proving to be much worse than even he had thought it might become.

Someone, and Stavros suspected who, had taken two dead snakes, wrapped them around a pole, and stuck it on her door. Done in the exact manner as the medical emblem—a caduceus—

the snakes' eyes had been grotesquely gouged out, turning them into something belonging only in a Halloween house of horrors.

Stavros wondered if Allie had seen the resemblance to her profession's insignia.

He hoped that she hadn't.

But as he held her close to him, it was the weight of his own lack of welcome toward her that was heaviest on his heart. She gave the impression of courage and strength, but at the moment, she felt so slight in his arms, so fragile. She was one woman, one slender woman, up against so much.

He knew there was a strength in her that was much greater than brawn. But that aside, he also knew it was time for him to get his emotions under control and to offer her the friendship that even Jeannie had noticed lacking in him: the friendship Allie needed in order to survive in this village.

But first, as a friend, he would try one more time to make her understand why Kastro wasn't the community she should make her home.

"Allie," he whispered her name again, and she seemed to relax. "I'm sorry, but I tried to warn you," he continued. "This village isn't the place for you. There's so much going on that you just can't understand—"

She stiffened against him, and he stopped speaking. She lifted her face from his chest and met his gaze straight on.

"Then tell me," she ground out. "When fighting a disease, a physician has to know the history of the patient. It's the same thing with this village. If I know what the root of this problem is, I can combat it." She looked deeply into his eyes. "Please, Stavros, tell me what's going on."

As he held her close, and gazed over her face, he knew, if he were honest with himself, that at that moment he admired everything about her. She was vulnerable and yet strong; she was proud and yet humble; she was professional and yet sensitive.

But mostly, she was a beautiful, smart woman who had asked for his help.

He knew then that he would give it to her.

Besides, he was almost certain that once she knew the truth, she would leave Kastro of her own accord, then he—well, he could get his feelings, as well as his well-planned life, back on track. But a small, nagging part of him wondered if it would even be possible for him to go back to before.

Cocking his head in the direction of the grisly display on the door, he said, "Poor beasts. They didn't deserve that." he sighed. "Let me get it cleaned up. Then we'll talk."

Relief seemed to fill her at his words, and on a shuddering sigh she admitted, "My fear of snakes rivals Indiana Jones's, from the Spielberg movies," she said, a forced smile curving her lips. "Even when they're just slithering across the ground, I'm pretty scared of them. But this"—she jutted her chin toward the unwelcome "gift"—"this was just too much for..." She paused, and he could tell she was wondering if she should continue. He was glad when she did. "This city girl."

Stavros squeezed her shoulders, and feeling as if their relationship was moving onto a different level, he motioned in the direction of the snakes and grimly admitted, "This would be too much for anybody." She blinked her eyes in obvious appreciation of his honesty, and he was glad he had spoken truthfully.

Then, with a bleakness, a sadness, in her voice that made his muscles bunch beneath his shoulders, she pronounced, "It's the caduceus—the physician's emblem."

He should have known that its symbolism wouldn't get by her. "I know," he replied and again felt that need, that desire, to protect her. Especially when he saw worry flicker through her eyes.

"What bothers me the most, though," she continued, "is the human snake who put it there."

That was what worried Stavros, too.

"Baba!" Jeannie's frightened voice called out from the kitchen window. "Is Yatrinna okay?"

"She's fine," he called over his left shoulder, and letting go of Allie, he bent down to collect her fallen groceries, trying to ignore how empty he felt no longer holding her. He nodded in the direction of his house. "Go sit with Jeannie while I get this cleaned up. We'll talk when I finish."

Her lips moved into a smile. It was one of thanks, flavored with relief. Stavros knew that was all she wanted to hear.

He saw a slight tremor behind the smile, but as she held out her hands to take the bags, he also noticed that her long, slender, healing fingers were steady.

Iron will, cotton-soft personality. That seemed to sum up Allie Alexander.

Inadvertently, a few minutes later, while in his kitchen, Stavros repeated Papouli's words of the previous day almost verbatim to Allie. "It's not that the villagers have anything against you personally."

But Allie wasn't buying it. Not today. Not after the snake attack. She slung her arm in the direction of her apartment door. "No? Well, it certainly seems as though somebody does," she shot out.

Stavros's chest lifted on a deep breath, and he shook his head slightly as he added ice to the *frappés*—iced coffees—which he had just poured for them. "No," he denied and turned to her. "It goes much deeper than that and," he said, pausing, his dark eyes nearly boring holes into her own, "it's much more dangerous."

"Dangerous?"

He nodded toward the door through which his daughter had just exited. "I sent Jeannie to her friend's house because I don't want her alarmed by what I have to tell you."

She dipped her chin in response, and he was surprised that for a change he wasn't bothered by that professional quality in her. She was cool, waiting, and rational. All characteristics—he realized with a start—that were needed to deal with the situation.

He drew a deep breath and, crossing over to the table, handed her a glass of frothy frappé before taking the seat opposite her. After a moment he asked, "Have you met Tasos Drakopoulos?"

When her mouth quirked distastefully downward, he had his answer. "Oh, yes. He and his wife have been most"—she paused, seeming to him to test different descriptions in her mind before settling on—"shall we say, hospitable."

"I'll bet they have," he answered with equal sarcasm, while wondering what sort of run-in she had had with the good mayor and his wife. "I believe that Drakopoulos is behind all this."

"I suspected as much. But why? Why does he seem to hate me so much?"

"It's not you he hates," Stavros said and picked up the salt shaker from the center of the table, "but the fact that you hold the position he wanted for his son." With a small thump, he placed the shaker next to its mate that was filled with pepper.

"His son?" Allie sat back, as though, Stavros thought, she

117

were trying to get a better angle on an X-ray. "A case of jealousy is the last thing I expected to hear."

Stavros stood, picked up his frappé, and walked over to the mantel. Turning back to Allie, he said, "Quite simply, Dimitri—Drakopoulos's son—is a recent medical school graduate, and Tasos wanted your job to go to him."

Allie shrugged her shoulders. "Then why didn't Dimitri put in for it? Depending upon availability, doctors can apply for whichever village or town they desire."

"I think that he did. But he did so too late or something." Taking a sip of his coffee, he continued, "Anyway, the way I understand it, the position had already been given to you."

"But how can I"—she lightly touched her hand to her chest—"be held responsible for Drakopoulos's son applying too late? And why is the entire village against me because of it?"

"It's not you they're against."

"Then who?"

"One another."

Frown lines appeared across the smoothness of her brow. "What?"

Stavros sat back down across from her and, after expelling a deep breath, asked, "Allie Alexander, haven't you realized yet that you've landed yourself in the middle of a feud?"

"A feud?" Allie's first thought was that it was a ridiculous notion. "I don't believe it!" Feuds didn't exist anymore except in far-off places that were away from the rest of the world—

She stopped her thought.

What was Kastro if not a far-off place away from the rest of the world?

There was a sardonic look in Stavros's eyes, which, for once, Allie knew she deserved. "I think, Doctor, that you have romanticized living in a Greek mountain village."

That was exactly what she had done, but there was no way she was going to admit it. With a throat that had suddenly gone dry, she stated, "Please explain about this feud." A feud wasn't something she wanted to deal with. But if she had to, she would, as long as she knew all the facts that had led up to it and where she stood in its history.

He picked up the pepper shaker and seemed to contemplate it for a moment before turning back to her. "Its origins are probably as old as the foundations of this village, going back deep into ancient times when one man ran off with another man's wife or some such equally romantic notion. The village has been divided into two camps made up of two main families for centuries." He held up the salt shaker. "The Drakopoulos family. And"—he held out the pepper shaker—"the Angelopoulos family." He knocked the tops of the shakers together, then set them on the table, a few inches between them.

Allie reached out and wiped the tip of her finger across the pepper that was stuck to the top of its container. Of their own accord her lips twitched. "Do their names by any chance imply their characters? The Draculas versus the Angels, maybe?"

Stavros chuckled, and Allie liked the twin dimples that appeared when he smiled. They matched the flash of sparkle in his eyes. "It might seem that way to you at the moment," Stavros wryly continued, "but even the Angelopouloses seem to be fallen angels on some occasions."

"Oh." She rolled her eyes and waited for him to continue. One thing the snakes on the pole had done was to bring them closer together as friends. Allie liked the feeling—a lot.

"Where you landed in this feud is really quite simple," he continued. "The only one in the village who had the connections with the Department of Health to ensure that the position would be reserved for Drakopoulos's son happened to be a member of the Angelopoulos family—"

"And he refused to help," Allie interjected.

Stavros nodded. "I'm impressed at how quickly you pick up on village politics."

"Why didn't he help?"

Stavros sighed. "This is the stickler. The Angelopouloses claimed that he did."

"You don't believe it?"

He shrugged his shoulders. "I don't know."

"Is there anything else that you can tell me about this situation?"

Stavros clicked his tongue against the inside of his cheek. "Just the same thing that I've said before. I don't think this is something you should settle into. You don't know how long it could go on or, for that matter, what they might do."

"Are you trying to scare me away?" she asked, but in spite of his words, she still felt as though they were on the same side.

"I'm not," he stated. "But somebody is."

"Mr. Andreas—"

"Stavros," he corrected her. "It seems a little redundant to go back to formalities after the crisis has passed."

She nodded. She wanted to be on a first-name basis with him. "Stavros, I've got one thing going for me that most rural doctors don't have."

He waited silently for her to finish.

"I want to be here."

"I'm glad," he said, surprising her. From the way his eyes widened, she suspected that his pronouncement surprised even him a bit. "The villages around here are remote, and they do need a doctor."

Allie squinted. "I"—she paused and licked her lips—"I mean, I was under the impression that you wanted me gone from here."

"I don't think Kastro is a place for a young woman on her own," he said, but she got the impression that there was much more to it than that. She was almost certain it had more to do with the feelings that bounced around them whenever they were together, emotions that were ready to take over even this conversation. "Especially with the feud."

She lifted her chin in challenge. "Isn't that a bit chauvinistic?"

"Maybe," he conceded, his tone clipped. "Look—life is tough enough in the city, but up here in the wilds"—he shrugged his shoulders—"it's wild."

She regarded him in silence for a moment as she thought about Dale—the forever-young boy in the framed pictures in her apartment, the boy on the threshold of manhood who had been caught in the cross fire of a supermarket holdup. "Believe me, Stavros, there are more animals in the city—in any city—than you will ever find in the country."

The faraway look in her eye told him she was speaking from experience rather than mouthing a cliché, and he wondered about it. But he still felt he had to try to convince her one more time to leave before things became any dirtier. "Allie, be realistic. We're talking about a feud. A real dispute. Not something Hollywood has dreamed up for modern man's enjoyment. But a dangerous civil battle that reaches centuries back into the very fabric of this village." He paused and spoke each word deliberately. "And you—are caught—in the middle—of it."

By way of answer, she gathered all her purchases, arose from her chair, and crossed over to the door. There she paused, and turning back to him, she lifted her chin a fraction and replied in the same measured tone he had used with her, "Then I—will just—have to figure out—how to break free."

And she left.

As the door closed behind her, Stavros wondered if he would ever break free of the hold she had on him.

Or—he took a thoughtful sip of his coffee—if he even wanted to.

Chapter 11—Broken Pump

An insistent knocking pounded within Allie's sleep-drugged brain, and as she willed her heavy eyelids to open, she realized the sound was knuckles hitting against the wooden door.

"Yatrinna? Are you in there?" The muffled sound of Jeannie's voice came to Allie above the racket of cicadas in the pine trees outside.

Fighting the gravity that seemed to be in cahoots with her weary limbs to keep her in bed, Allie pulled herself up and walked on leaden feet to the kitchen for a glass of well water. "Come on in," she croaked out after the first sip. "It's open."

Jeannie pushed the door wide, and Allie smiled when she saw how the girl was dressed. She had on white coveralls and a white T-shirt, while her hair was tied back in a painter's kerchief. A whitewasher's brush slung over her shoulder completed the ensemble.

Allie lifted the glass away from her lips. "My, don't you look like a professional painter," she commented with a twinkle in her eye.

Jeannie's lips quirked, a kid's combination smile of both pride and shyness. "It was the only way Baba would allow me to whitewash," she explained, motioning down at her clothes. "He said it wouldn't matter if he couldn't get it out since it was the same color."

Allie lifted her eyebrows at that. Stavros had learned how to think like a mother concerned with the laundry, but with an added flare. Allie seriously doubted that most mothers would think to color coordinate the paint with the clothes. "What a smart father you have," she commented, and splashing her face with water from the kitchen faucet, she padded over to the antique mirror that hung above the dresser to brush out her hair.

Leaning the whitewasher's brush in the corner by the door, Jeannie walked up next to her as she styled her hair in a single French braid. "How can you do that by yourself?" She was in awe of Allie's skillful fingers as they flew over her head.

"Well," Allie paused, "since my mother died when I was just a little girl—"

"My mother died, too," Jeannie interrupted, and Allie's fingers stilled as she looked at the girl in the mirror. She had been under the impression that Jeannie's parents had been divorced. Thinking back, though, she realized that had never been said. "But it was like she was dead even when she was alive," Jeannie continued, as if she were talking about the weather. "I mean, she never lived with Baba and me, and I never saw her." Allie understood then why she had had the impression of divorce. But she also realized now that Stavros Andreas's life was much more complicated than she had thought.

"I'm sorry…about your mother."

"It's not your fault," Jeannie said with total logic. But Allie understood that even though Jeannie had experienced two of the most devastating things a child could go through—the breakup of her parents' marriage, plus the death of her mother—Stavros had brought his daughter through them both unscathed. She was coming to admire him more with each thing she learned about him.

But Jeannie was only interested in Allie's hair. Pointing to it, she asked, "Did your father teach you to do that?"

Allie resumed braiding and smiled at the thought of her

dear father and his thick fingers trying to fix her hair. "No. He didn't even know how to put it in a simple braid or ponytail."

"He didn't?" Jeannie touched the tip of her ponytail, which peeked out from under the kerchief. "My baba fixes my hair."

Allie smiled. "He does a great job."

"But not even he can do it like that." She motioned to the way Allie took small clumps of hair from the side and added them to those at the back. "But I don't think anyone in the village can. Maybe Natalia, but she's gone now." Jeannie was quick to defend her father.

"Well, I'll fix your hair like this whenever you want me to," Allie offered and was rewarded with a smile almost as wide as the valley outside the window.

"Really?"

"Sure!" She tied the end of the braid with a small ribbon, slid her feet into her flip-flops, and, squeezing Jeannie close to her, said, "Now, come on. We've got a clinic to paint!"

Martha was waiting for them with all the necessary paraphernalia. Among the three of them, they managed to whitewash the interior of the office and waiting room within a little more than two hours. It smelled fresh and clean, and Allie had the deep satisfaction of knowing that she would be able to set up her medical supplies in the morning and open the clinic for patients by the following evening.

Even after all the years of working and living in Greece, she still had a hard time getting used to the working hours. But remembering the afternoon heat and lack of air conditioning, she thought it brilliant. People left their offices at about half past one, went home for lunch and a snooze, and then returned to work in the cool of the evening. Allie hadn't been surprised to learn that the custom stretched back to ancient days.

"It hardly seems like the same place as this morning," Allie commented to Martha. They watched together as Jeannie finished the final section of the last wall.

Martha laughed and pointed to Allie's hair, arms, and face. "And neither do you!"

Allie looked down at her body and touched her cheek where her skin felt pulled by the whitewash that had landed there. One glance at Martha showed her to be spotless. Even Jeannie had less paint on her than Allie had gotten on herself. "How do you two manage to do it so neatly?"

Martha laughed again while, in the quick manner Allie was becoming accustomed to in the small woman, she hurriedly folded the sheet that had been protecting the desk. "Years of practice. We whitewash our homes every spring. Now"—she speedily moved on to another subject—"Kyria Maria will come in the morning and fix the wicker in the chairs, and Kyrios Pavlos will fix the broken furniture, and whatever upholstery can't be fixed, I will cover with pillows and material."

Allie would have told Martha how much she appreciated all her help if Martha had allowed her to get a word in. But Martha continued to speak with the speed of a Formula One racer. "And it will all look beautiful!" Standing in the connecting doorway, she surveyed the rooms as if seeing them completed already. "I will come in the morning and make sure everything is done properly, but I must be going home now—"

"I'm done!" Jeannie interrupted, standing back to look at the wall she had painted.

Martha took a quick moment to glance at it. "It's beautiful, Jeannie." Then, turning, she practically ran out of the office. "See you both tomorrow!"

"Bye, and thanks again," Allie called after her, but Martha

was already on the road heading toward her house. Allie walked over to stand next to Jeannie as the girl continued to admire her work. There was pride in what she had accomplished, a good and healthy pride for something real and visible.

"It looks terrific!" Allie commended her, but when she would have pulled Jeannie into a congratulatory hug, the girl caught a glimpse of her paint-smeared body and stepped away laughing.

"Yatrinna! You're a mess!"

Allie looked down at herself and laughed, too. "I am, aren't I?"

Jeannie rolled her eyes. "Boy! Am I glad I don't look like that. My father wouldn't like it." As her parent chose that moment to walk into the office, she shouted out, "Baba!" Taking his hand, Jeannie drew him up to face her masterpiece. "Look! I did this wall all by myself!"

Stavros put his hand on her shoulder and glanced over at Allie. But seeing her appearance, his eyes widened, and Allie was sure she saw something like amused admiration flash into them, definitely not the aversion Jeannie had said he would feel, before he turned back to his waiting daughter to comment on her paint job.

"It's beautiful." His gaze danced merrily toward Allie. "But are you responsible for putting the white in our new doctor's hair?"

The girl's eyes widened like shiny marbles. "No! I didn't—"

Allie pulled her paint-speckled braid in front of her eyes to see just how bad it was. It looked like the trunk of a polka-dotted, stuffed elephant. "No." Allie laughed, as she slung the braid back behind her. "I managed to do it all by myself." As Stavros regarded her, the deep brown coloring of his eyes turned soft and glossy, and something in Allie's heart did a flip-flop.

"I think it's very becoming," he finally said.

Allie glanced over at Jeannie and smiled the smile of a female sure that another, no matter how young, would understand. "Well, becoming or not, I must admit that I can't wait to soak all the sweat and paint of this day away in a nice long bath," she admitted, thinking with longing about the elegant bathtub that awaited her. She wouldn't forget to put the IN USE sign under the Andreas's door this time, either.

But when Stavros turned back to her, she immediately saw that friendship was gone. In its light and happy place was once again the opaqueness of doubt and challenge. Allie cringed.

"Well, I'm afraid you're going to have to do without that bath," he stated sharply.

Her brows came together in a questioning frown. She had the uncanny feeling he was testing her somehow. "What do you mean?"

"The water pump is broken."

"Oh, no!" Jeannie wailed out, swiveling her face up to her father. "Not again."

"Yes, again," he answered his daughter. "And this time I've had to order a part from Athens in order to fix it." He glanced back at Allie. "It will be at least a week, maybe even more, before it's repaired."

"Until then?" Allie asked, as sweat trickled down her back, reminding her of just how in need she was of a bath. "What do we do?"

He shrugged his shoulders. "Either we use the garden hose and have an icy cold rinse in the garden, do without or"—he paused, and there was no doubt in Allie's mind that there was challenge in the timbre of his voice now—"we lug the water up from the faucet in the garden and fill up the bathtub. I have an immersion heater that warms the water just fine."

"Ugh," Allie groaned. Having a nice hot soak in that marble bathtub at the end of the day had kept her aching arm moving the brush back and forth, especially during the last hour. Absently, she rubbed her shoulders. "How many pails does it require?"

"About twenty."

"Twenty!" she gasped.

"I'll help you, Yatrinna," Jeannie offered.

Allie glanced at the girl and smiled. "You've been the biggest helper in this village. Thanks, but I'll manage."

"I don't mind," Jeannie insisted.

"I do. I know you have plans with Eva, and I won't let you break them."

"Okay, but will you come to dinner tonight?" Jeannie asked and looked up at her father expectantly.

Jeannie had asked Allie earlier, but Allie had been vague in answering, not knowing if the invitation had really come from the girl's father as well. She turned her gaze to his.

"I've made *yemistes*—stuffed tomatoes." He surprised her by encouraging her to come and share a stuffed tomato dinner with them. But she knew the reason why. Jeannie. Jeannie was his Achilles' heel. He would do almost anything for his daughter.

"Mmm...sounds delicious." A lot better than the cheese, bread, and olives that was to be dinner at her house. "But I can't. Not tonight." At the disappointed sigh that came from Jeannie, Allie quickly suggested to the girl, "Maybe tomorrow night?"

"But why?" Jeannie persisted.

"Jeannie," Stavros admonished her.

But Allie didn't mind explaining. "I'm exhausted, Jeannie.

And I must have a bath." She looked over at the girl's father. "So I'm afraid I'll be rather busy."

***

Half an hour later, Stavros heard Allie lug the last two pails of water up the seventeen stairs. He had counted every time she had carried the sloshing buckets past his door. Twenty pails of water, carrying two pails at a time, meant she had made ten trips. On trip numbers three, seven, and nine, he had almost gone out to help her, but he had stopped himself each time. The last time, his hand had been on the doorknob, his knuckles white from tension.

It wasn't that he was lazy or that he didn't want to help her, because he did. It would have been a whole lot easier if he had filled up the tub. But he had convinced himself that to do so would be to do her a disservice.

She had to learn how hard life in a remote village could be now, while she could still get away. Under the best of circumstances, living in Kastro would be hard for a city dweller, and she wasn't even there under good conditions. The feud made sure of that. A broken water pump was the least on a long list of problems that could occur.

He sighed with relief when he heard her leave the empty pails outside her front door. He hadn't expected her to carry the water from the garden up to the bathroom. He had thought for sure she would balk at the idea. Then, during trip number five, he had been sure she would opt for a partial bath instead of the real thing.

She hadn't. Even when her footsteps had faltered with exhaustion. He had never admired such iron will in a person when she continued.

And a few moments later, when the IN USE sign was shoved under his door and he heard the bathroom door click shut, he grabbed an apple from the bowl and strode across the room to his door.

While Allie splashed around in the tub he would go and visit Charger.

Maybe he'd stay there all night.

Chapter 12—An Ally

Crash!

Allie's eyes flew open, and she shot up in bed. In the soft light of the street lamp, her focusing eyes saw that one of the French windows was gone. In the place of the smooth glass were knives of crystal sticking out from its edges, looking like a computer game's torture zone.

A storm was raging outside, not the normal kind that brought rain and wet but, rather, the dry, windy kind. One that pushed its way though the broken glass like a vortex—but of air, not water—and whipped her long, silky hair around her face in a wild and savage abandonment.

She reached for the bedside lamp. Click. Nothing happened. All remained dark. Click, click, click, she frantically tried the lamp again, her eyes opening wide in fear. But nothing. There was no electricity.

"Allie!" She heard Stavros call out, and relief washed through her. She wasn't alone. Stavros was in the central hall.

"Stavros!" she called back, glad that she managed to keep the terror that had begun to seep into her system out of her voice. "It's unlocked." Thankfully, she had forgotten to lock it the last time she had used the bathroom. "Come in, but be careful. There's broken glass."

"I'll put some shoes on and be right back."

He was gone for only a moment. When he entered, a beam of light, blessed light, preceded him into the room, and nothing, and no one, had ever looked so good to her.

Wearing untied hiking boots, he crunched across the floor

toward her. With his bare chest and cut-off jeans, he resembled a road worker—a super good-looking one—during the heat of a summer day. "What happened?" he demanded, his voice husky from sleep.

She shrugged her shoulders and pointed at the broken window. "I'm not sure…" A gust of wind slammed a shutter in his part of the house, and glancing toward the sound, she offered, "Maybe a branch broke it?"

In the dim light of the battery-operated torch, she saw his mouth angle into a frown. "There aren't any trees up front." His answer was clipped as he sent the light around the glass-littered room. "Where are your shoes?" he asked when she remained quiet.

She grimaced and motioned toward the broken window. "I put them over there last night."

The beam of light located her yellow flip-flops, summer sandals, and running shoes. They were as she'd left them, all in a neat row under the window—now, however, with shards of glass glimmering in and all around them. "Do you have others?"

"I have hiking boots." She motioned toward a large suitcase in the far corner of the living room. "But I haven't unpacked them yet."

Before she knew what was happening, he bent down and put one arm around her back while the other easily went beneath her knees. "What are you doing?" she asked and frantically smoothed her nightgown down.

"I learned years ago never to go through a woman's suitcase," he explained as her arms instinctively found their way around his neck, while her face settled against his shoulder. He smelled good, like summer sun and honey, but he felt even better, sinewy and strong, with muscles that easily held her weight.

He looked down at her, and their eyes met. His head slowly descended toward hers; hers slowly ascended to his. Their mouths touched in a sweet kiss that was wondrous and lovely because both wonder and, amazingly, love were in it.

Allie had only loved the boy in the picture who stared smiling up at them from a decade past on her bedside table. But he had only been a boy, and she an even younger girl. Although she had dated sporadically, as much as medical school and residency permitted, she had never felt this way with a man before. Stavros awakened feelings in her that she had thought were only to be found in fiction, in fairy tales.

After the sweet kiss ended, he gently, softly carried her into the living area. There, as if she were the most precious woman in the world, he lowered her to the floor.

He smiled.

She smiled.

When his dimples flashed in his cheeks, she knew he was going to speak. "You're quite a woman, Dr. Allie Alexander."

Suddenly feeling shy, she stepped away from him to open her suitcase. Stavros looked uncomfortable, as well, and he turned and walked back toward the sleeping alcove.

Allie found her hiking boots and put them on. Crunching her way toward Stavros, who was standing at the base of her bed, she saw he was examining something in his hand. He turned and held up a tennis ball–sized rock. "Now we know what broke the window."

She reached out for the rock and felt its weight in her hand, while he glanced over to where her head had been on her pillow, just a scant five feet from where the rock had landed. "It could have hurt you badly had it hit you."

"It could have," she conceded and grimaced. "But it didn't," she reminded him. "And I don't think the purpose of throwing the rock was to hurt me. Just to scare me."

"I agree. But I still don't think this is a good situation for you to be in."

"I'm not leaving," she returned.

They regarded one another, adversaries, and yet not.

Letting out a deep breath, Stavros turned and moved over to the desk. He lit the lantern he had brought when he entered the apartment. He picked up the book she had left on the desk and snorted. "Collection of Classic Fairy Tales? Do you read this stuff?"

She stiffened. "I like fairy tales."

"I don't even think fairy tales are good for children," he stated and glanced back up at her before dropping the book, none too gently, onto the desk. Even with the wind blowing hard and loud, the thump it made hitting the wood of the desk could be heard. "But at least now I understand why you aren't realistic in your expectations."

Her eyebrows shot up. "I'm not realistic? Stavros, if there is one thing being a physician does, it's to make realists out of people."

He glanced toward the collection of stories again. A Bible and a Physicians' Desk Reference were stacked beside it. He shook his head, then motioned toward the broken window and the rock she still held in her hand. "I suspect you're going to need a fairy godmother to get you out of this mess."

She remembered thinking about Papouli in that way—as her fairy godfather. But even more than that wonderful man, she needed her faith. "Actually, Stavros," she said, and walking over to the desk, she put down the rock and picked up her Bible. "I think all I need is the confidence that I am right where God wants me to be. That's a faith that enables me to commit my way to the Lord and to trust in Him even when men"—she pointed to the rock—"carry out their wicked schemes."

A sound, something more a close cousin to a snicker than to a laugh, emanated from him as he glanced down at the Bible in her hands. "Do you really believe that God cares about you?"

"Absolutely." She didn't allow even a moment's hesitation in her response. "'In all things God works for the good *of those who love him*,'" she said, reciting part of Romans 8:28. "I love Him, so it follows that He cares for me—very much."

"Now *that's* a fairy tale," he huffed out.

She picked up her book of fairy tales. "No, these are fairy tales." She raised the Bible in her right hand higher. "What's written in here"—she paused for emphasis—"is Truth." She pointed to the array of icons on the wall above the desk that depicted some of the greatest Christians who had ever lived. St. Nikolaos and St. Paul were two of them. "It's what they believed, too."

"You are as they were—idealist."

Allie didn't challenge him. What she did was scrutinize him, just as she might a patient when she was endeavoring to put together all the symptoms for a diagnosis. "You know what I think, Stavros? I think that in actual fact *you* are the idealist; an idealist of the most dangerous kind. You are one whose ideals have been shattered."

He waved his hand in front of him as if he were swatting away the notion like a fly. "That's ridiculous."

"Is it?" He didn't respond, so she continued. "You know, it's not an uncommon ailment. Many people, most people, actually," she qualified, "tend to blame God when things don't go their way, when life throws them a curve ball." She smiled wryly and looked down. "Or a rock. The thing is, most people quite quickly understand the fallacy of their thinking."

His upper lip twisted in a sardonic smile. "You know, Dr. Alexander, I find this a rather amazing topic, particularly since you're the one who was just attacked."

"Why is it amazing? It just proves that I'm not an idealist. I know human nature well. I'll admit that it would have been pleasant to have been welcomed to Kastro nicely and that it was a bit of a shock when I wasn't." She shrugged her shoulders. "But I've lived through worse things. I'll get through this." She placed the Bible back on her desk, lovingly running her fingertips over its cover before training her gaze on Stavros. "Particularly with God's Word to guide me."

He held up his hands in a halting gesture. "I tell you what, Allie, I'll live life my way, and you live life your way."

She smiled. "Not my way, Stavros. God's way. If I were living life my way, well, let's just say I never would have made it to Kastro. Not as its doctor, anyway."

He motioned toward the lantern, effectively stopping their discussion. "I'll leave that for you." Then he nodded his head toward the street lamp. "The rest of the village has lights."

She swiveled her head toward the streetlight that cut through the dark of the country night. "You mean—"

He finished for her. "We're the only house without power."

"They cut the wire?"

Stavros shrugged his shoulders. "That would be my guess."

Allie sighed, then collapsed onto the edge of the sofa. "Should I call the police?" she asked after a moment.

"If you want to, but this is a *village* feud with a jurisdiction all its own. Unless someone gets hurt, the police aren't normally involved."

"Do people normally get hurt?"

"No," he said. "In this day and age it's more psychological."

She sighed. "I thought as much."

A gust of wind rattled the loose daggers of crystal that stuck out of the window frame in the bedroom. Motioning back toward it, he said, "Let me help you clean up—"

"No." She patted the sofa. "I'll sleep the rest of the night here and pick it up in the morning."

"I don't mind."

She held up her hand. "I do. I'm too tired to clean it now." Her gaze went to Dale's photo.

"Who is he?" Stavros's voice sounded sharp.

She glanced back up at him before returning her attention to the picture. Leaning over, she gently ran her fingertips across the smooth image of the boy, the boy who was almost a man. "We were childhood sweethearts. I was going to marry him. We were going to go to medical school together, set up a practice in rural America, and live…happily-ever-after."

"What happened?"

Allie turned. "About ten years ago he was a casualty of the wild city." She paused and explained. "He was caught in the cross fire of a supermarket holdup."

Stavros's face softened. "I'm sorry," he murmured.

Allie sighed, a sound heavy with the evening's event and memories of Dale's death. "Thanks again for your help," she said, hoping he would understand she needed to be alone.

But he didn't. Stavros ran the light beam back toward the broken glass. "Let me clean it up. You don't have to do anything."

"I'll do it in the morning."

The muscles around his mouth tightened. "Allie—"

She held up her hand to stop him. "I'm not leaving," she lashed out, but blinked when all he did was smile.

"I was just going to say, there are good people in Kastro and people who need the care you have to offer. Just give it a little bit of time."

"Does that mean you don't want me to leave?" she ventured to ask.

"I still don't think Kastro is the place for you." He pointed in the direction of the broken glass. "This proves it." He paused. "I just want you to know, though, that since you aren't going to leave, you can count on me to help you in any way you need."

Relieved, she smiled. "Thanks. That means a lot to me."

Stavros smiled back, as if to say it meant a lot to him, as well.

Chapter 13—Ultimatum

Allie awoke in the morning to a wind that was, if anything, even stronger, hotter, and drier than it had been throughout the eventful night.

But it wasn't the wind she was thinking about. It was the kiss she had shared with Stavros, a kiss that she knew must not be repeated. She couldn't, wouldn't, do anything to jeopardize her professional integrity.

She had already gone through that once. And it had been a false charge.

She might be able to handle gossip if she knew for a fact that there was nothing to it, that they had no more affection for one another than just simple friendship. But—she let out a deep breath of resignation, a breath she hadn't even realized she'd been holding—they were already past that point.

She slid her fingertips over her lips.

The midnight rock thrower had seen to that. He'd done much more than toss a rock through her window; he'd thrown the two of them together, as well.

Shoving her feet into her boots, she clomped over to the refrigerator for a glass of cold orange juice. The power was still off, so it was only slightly chilled, but it was refreshing. As the liquid relieved her parched throat and its natural sugar filled her veins with energy, she knew what she had to do, or rather, could not do.

She couldn't allow herself to be anything more than friends with Stavros.

Nothing else.

No more kissing, no more touching.

Friends.

Platonic friends.

Period.

She took a deep breath.

Period.

With that problem intellectually solved, she quickly swept up the broken glass, cleaned her shoes and dressed in a summer dress of pale lemon for her day at the clinic.

But when, a little while later, she stepped out her front door and saw Stavros balancing high above her head on a ladder, she recognized how irrational intellectual decrees were in the face of the emotionalism that surrounded the two of them.

He was fixing the cut power cable.

She wished he could cut the emotional one that sang to life between them every time they looked at one another—sever it in two, and in turn sever the halves. But she doubted it was possible. They were conductors of a kind of power that would always zap to life when they were in the same room together. Charged atmosphere.

Highly dangerous.

But nice.

Stavros's gaze found hers. He held up the two ends of the neatly sliced cable. She knew that he was warning her to be careful.

Squaring her shoulders, she nodded and walked toward the stairs. She was aware of his gaze following her.

When she turned the corner and knew he could no longer see her, she paused and scanned the red-tiled roofs of the village. She knew now that its apparent peacefulness was false. There was no peace in the world, and there was no peace in the remote village of Kastro, either. She looked up at the castle. With it sitting high above the town, guarding it, she should have known better. Castles weren't built for romance; they were built for protection.

She sighed and looked back down over the village. Her gaze settled on the gaily painted blue shutters of the priest's home. The word *peace* entered her mind, but this time in a positive way. His home was a haven of warmth, friendship, and godly love. She smiled, gladdened by what she had found there. Her fairy godfather. But no, Papouli was much better. Her gaze shifted over to the ceramic tiles of the old Byzantine chapel next to his home. He was the real thing. A true agent of God.

Allie's lips moved a moment before words formed and came out. "Lord, I ask You in Your precious Son Jesus' name to please help me," she finally whispered. It was a simple prayer, not unlike millions prayed to the Lord during the previous two millennia. But because she believed so strongly in God's loving care, it was powerful—probably fourteen of the best words humans could ever speak. Like so many believers before her, both in this village and around the world, Allie was confident God would indeed come to her aid. With footsteps now lighter after casting her cares on her heavenly Father, Allie walked down the stairs and into the heart of the village.

When Allie turned into the clinic's walkway a few minutes later and saw the tortoise on his back—his short legs flailing in a futile effort to right himself—and the door to the clinic pounding in the strong wind, she knew her prayer for God's help was one she would repeat again and again. She righted the tortoise, taking a moment to place it in a protective corner next to a bowl of water, and turned to face the ominous black that was behind the unlatched door. She had left it closed and locked the previous evening. Someone with a key must have paid it a visit.

Allie thought she knew who.

She reached out her hand, tentatively pushed back the door, flipped the light switch, and gasped.

The office had been trashed, ruined, vandalized. It looked like the very people who had given the word meaning, the Vandals of the early Middle Ages, had swept through, leaving malicious destruction and chaos in their wake. The walls that Martha, Jeannie, and she had so painstakingly whitewashed the previous evening were smeared with graffiti, reminding Allie of an uncared for section of a city.

Allie got mad. Really mad.

Not taking the time to even turn off the light, she left the office as she had found it, with the door pounding in the wind, and strode purposefully through the village toward the *kafenion*.

She had had enough.

She might have unwittingly landed herself in the middle of an archaic feud, but that didn't mean she had to remain a passive player.

If they wanted to play hardball, she would, too. She was from New York City, USA. She knew how to.

The courtyards and homes were buzzing with villagers battening down their belongings against the high winds. They saw Allie—and her demeanor—as she passed, and with innate village curiosity, many followed, or in the case of several *yiayias*—grandmothers—sent grandchildren after her to see what was happening.

The sour-faced Dionysia's gasp registered in Allie's mind as she went into the *kafenion*, but she didn't have the patience to give the pathetic woman more than a glance. Marching right up to Tasos Drakopoulos's table, Allie slammed the palm of her hand upon it. She didn't care in the least that she caused the three demitasses of coffee to slosh their brown liquid over their rims.

"I'm not leaving," she said without preamble, her voice hard.

Drakopoulos smiled a slow, smirking smile, which confirmed Allie's suspicions. He was behind everything—the snakes on her door, the rock throwing, and the clinic being trashed. There was no doubt in her mind.

"You're not wanted here," he said, repeating his very first words to her on the day she arrived in Kastro. But now Allie had a history of the disease that had infiltrated this village, and she knew how to fight it.

"The clinic had better be cleaned and painted before noon and in the shape it was before you vandalized it, or I'll contact the Department of Health and let them know what's going on here." Allie had the satisfaction of seeing Drakopoulos blanch. From her peripheral vision, she saw all the men in the *kafenion* swivel their heads around as they looked at one another. She had their attention—100 percent. Feeling more like a lawyer in a courtroom than a doctor, she continued. "If not, the Department of Health will withdraw the honor and privilege Kastro has in being the seat of the Rural Physician Clinic for this area. It will go to one of your neighboring villages."

There was a gasp from her audience, a sound that echoed out the cafe's doors as her words were repeated to the waiting ears of the villagers beyond. Allie knew she had hit a soft spot in village politics. She had been counting on the notorious rivalry of Greeks, one that had its roots in the ancient Hellenic city-states, when neighboring cities fought each other over everything and anything. She had thought there must be a village in the area that was coveting Kastro's medical clinic.

149

Now she was certain.

Without another word, without a muscle moving in her face, she turned and walked out the door.

At noon, when she checked in at the clinic, she would be certain.

Until then. . .

She would go to her apartment, get down on her knees, and pray.

Chapter 14—Perseverance

When Allie returned to the clinic at noon, refreshed by her prayer time and ensuing nap—one that helped her recapture some of the sleep she had lost during the night—she knew her diagnosis of the situation had been correct. The people of Kastro didn't want to lose the Rural Physician Clinic—even if it meant she was the one to run it. They had been frightened into action.

She found the clinic spotless, if possible even better than Martha, Jeannie, and she had left it the previous night.

The walls had been scrubbed of the graffiti and beautifully re-whitewashed, and the floor, polished by a professional machine this time, was so shiny it looked as though it belonged in the marble halls of a stately mansion, not in a lowly medical clinic in the middle of nowhere. About ten women were busy finishing up, but when Allie saw who was overseeing the entire operation, lines of displeasure formed on her forehead and part of her wished she hadn't challenged the Men's Club.

Out of the examining room, supporting her tummy with one hand, holding a bucketful of some sort of blue solution with the other while instructing a woman in how to clean the stain out of the sink, waddled dear, sweet Sophia Drakopoulos. In that unguarded moment, the sagging of her eyelids spoke clearly as to just how exhausted Sophia actually was. Allie was dismayed to think that Sophia had been working since early morning. This hot office was the last place any pregnant woman should be. Allie needed to examine her to be certain, but she suspected that Sophia was suffering from a combination of exhaustion and the heat. She hoped there wasn't anything else.

"Sophia," Allie called out, and the other woman's china doll face lit up when she turned and saw Allie.

"Yatrinna." Sophia held out her right hand in greeting. "I was so sorry when I heard what happened." She looked around the room with a satisfied expression in her blue eyes. "But I think"—her voice was barely above a breathless whisper—"you must agree that the women have put everything right once again."

Allie glanced around the room, and her eyes took in all the extras that had been added. Potted plants, a rubber tree and a palm, the upholstery all mended, two new chairs, paintings on the walls, and even a new cabinet in the examining room—something Allie was relieved to discover, because she had wondered where she was going to store her multitude of supplies. The latest editions of various magazines were on the coffee table in the waiting room, and she'd noticed when she walked in that even the garden had been spruced up. The rosebushes had been trimmed, the soil beneath them tilled, while reaching bougainvillea had been planted elegantly beside the window in perfect Mediterranean balance. The air of neglect had been totally erased from the little building, and the office was, in essence, as it should have been the day Allie arrived.

But she didn't say that to Sophia. She didn't want the dear lady to feel bad. "It's perfect." Then, looking over Sophia with a doctor's eye, she admonished, "But you have no business being here."

Sophia waved her concern aside. "I just heard today about how terrible the office was when you first arrived. I'm sorry, Yatrinna. I would have cleaned it had I known."

"Then I'm glad that you didn't know," Allie said without pause, because she was sure that without her threat Sophia would have been the only one doing the cleaning. "You must go home and rest. This heat is too much for all of us, but for you— and that child you're carrying—"

Allie's voice trailed off as Sophia made a circular, dismissing motion with her hand and sweetly cut in. "We village women are made of hardy stock, Yatrinna."

Allie frowned. It was her opinion that village women were strong, but to the detriment of their health, most walked in their early forties with what she'd labeled the "village waddle." Too many winter days out in the rain tending animals, washing clothes, cooking in wood-burning ovens, and a multitude of other things had sent arthritis to their hips at young ages. Allie took the bucket of solution from Sophia's hand and, with a smile, handed it to a passing woman, while guiding Sophia toward the door. "Hardy or not, you're going home now and to bed. Doctor's orders."

Sophia held her face up for the air to touch it. "Even with this wind, it is hot," she admitted and turned to Allie with a tired smile. "A nap does sound good," she further acknowledged, rubbing her hand across the bottom of her protruding tummy.

Allie knew that the only reason she conceded to rest was for the sake of the baby she so badly desired. "I want to examine you tomorrow," she pressed while Sophia seemed to be in the right mood.

Sophia smiled and wearily nodded. "Tomorrow," she agreed. Allie watched as Sophia waved to the rest of the women, then walked heavily up the winding road toward her house.

When Allie turned back to the clinic, she sighed. For some nagging reason—probably the fact that she didn't know much about Sophia's medical history—her condition bothered her.

As she watched the women pack their cleaning supplies and paraphernalia, sending her shy glances and hesitant smiles as they walked out the door, Allie was certain of one thing: There were more nice women like Sophia in the village.

A whole lot more.

That gave Allie hope.

Because of her late morning nap, Allie didn't sleep during the heat of the day. She finished unpacking her suitcases, then spent the afternoon in the shade of her vine-covered veranda reading a traveler's handbook on the history of Greece.

She had just finished reading about Minoan Crete and the Mycenaean civilization on the mainland and their famous Trojan War and was about to start on archaic Greece and the rise of the city-states, when the spicy scent of roasting chicken wafted in the wind that ruffled her pages.

Her stomach growled.

Oregano and pepper scented the air, and she lifted her head and sniffed as Jeannie's adorable little Siamese cat might. She hadn't realized how hungry she was.

Weighing her book down with a ceramic pot to keep it from taking flight, she went into the kitchen to see what she had to eat.

A can of sardines and a box of breakfast cereal were in the cupboard, while eggs, yogurt, and milk graced the shelves of the refrigerator. Nice food, but definitely not ideal for lunch and supper every day. She closed the fridge with a small kick. The time had finally come for her to learn how to cook. Her father and brother had done all the cooking while she was growing up, and her aunt when she'd been in medical school. After that, Allie had eaten most of her meals at the hospital or had called out. As she padded back out to the veranda, it suddenly occurred to her she wouldn't be able to call out for food in Kastro. She had to learn to cook now. There was no choice.

She wanted to. It was something basic, something real, and as the aroma drifted on the wind to her nose once again, she wondered if maybe she should follow the scent and see if that housewife might be convinced to teach her.

Sighing, she picked up her history book again and read how the country of Hellas came to be known as Greece. That had always intrigued her. When asked his nationality, a person from the country would not say he was Greek, but rather, that he was *Ellanas* if a man, or *Elannitha* if a woman.

Allie laughed when she read that the words Greece and Greek were actually derived from misunderstandings. When Hellenic colonists met the people in what is now known as southern Italy and were asked where they came from, they gave the name of their small city, Graia, rather than the overall area of Hellas.

It stuck.

From then on, the Hellenes became known in Latin as Graeci—the people of Graia—rather than the correct Hellenes. Thus came into being the adjective and noun *Greek*, or *Grecian*, while the name of the country became known as Greece abroad, instead of the correct Hellas.

But as she started reading about ancient Sparta, the most military-oriented society of ancient Hellas, Allie's stomach again interrupted her as her nose registered the scent of frying zucchini.

Zucchini was her favorite vegetable in the world, a culinary feast, and Allie hadn't eaten any in a very long time. Her mouth salivated.

That would be the first thing she'd learn to cook, she

decided, as she ignored her tummy and continued to read. She was into chapter five, having read about the glory of Ancient Athens, *Athena*; the Persian Wars; and the original marathon run, when there was a knock on her door.

Padding on bare feet across the wooden floor, she glanced at her watch and was startled to see it was nearly six. But when she opened the door, she was given a much greater surprise.

Alone and smiling stood Stavros.

"Hi," he said, and there was a shy tone to his voice that almost confounded her.

"Hi," she returned softly, his shyness contagious.

"I've come bringing a peace offering."

"As long as it isn't a wooden horse," Allie quickly quipped. But at his questioning look, she dipped her head and explained, "I've been reading Greek history all afternoon."

"Ah," he said, "the famous wooden horse of the Trojan War from which we get the expression 'Beware of Greeks bearing gifts.' " He chuckled. "A true military feat of genius," he commented and smiled. "But no. Unlike the Trojan horse, the gift this Greek American offers is genuine. A picnic dinner."

"A picnic?" Allie repeated and blinked. But when her tummy chose that moment to voice its desire, they both laughed, sharing in friendship.

Waving his hand down toward the rumble, he said, "I think I've just been given my answer."

"You most definitely have," she admitted. "When is this picnic to take place?" It touched her deeply that he had asked her out.

"In about fifteen minutes?"

She nodded again and moved to step back into her home when he motioned down to her bare feet. "Oh, and wear tennis shoes or hiking boots."

"Boots?"

He nodded. "I thought we'd go up to the castle."

"The castle?" She glanced up with trepidation at the low vegetation along the path leading up to the gaping entrance of the citadel. Most of it was dried a beautiful gold in the heat of the August earth, with only cactus to add bits of green. "But aren't there snakes up there?"

He chuckled, a sound that was more like a verbal caress than a laugh. "I think, darling Allie, that you've found more snakes down here than you will ever see up there," he replied, and she knew he had heard about her latest problem. Her spine stiffened as she readied herself for a fight. She didn't want to hear his opinion on her living in, or rather leaving, Kastro again. But when she saw the definite flicker of admiration in the shining darkness of his eyes, the armor within her slowly dismantled.

"But if we do run into snakes, darling Allie," he continued with admiration in his tone, "fearful or not, I feel sure you will know how to handle them." Chuckling lightly, a low sound Allie definitely liked, he turned and went around the veranda toward the door of his house.

Allie stood for a moment at her door even after he had disappeared around the corner. She couldn't believe he had complimented her. Nor that he had invited her out for a picnic dinner.

Her clinic was all cleaned and ready to be set up in the morning, and now this.

Kastro, she thought as she looked up at the castle that was glowing pink in the evening sun, was getting to be friendlier and friendlier.

And hadn't Stavros called her "darling Allie"?

Not once, but twice?

Maybe the prince of the bus was finally replacing the toad of the house. But she slowly shook her head as she closed the door.

Stavros had never been a toad.

Not ever.

Chapter 15—Picnic in the Castle

The path up to the castle was steep.

But it was also fragrant and thought-provoking, and Allie soon forgot all about snakes, both the variety that slither on the ground and the two-legged kind, as she followed Stavros up the zigzagging path.

The quiet of the medieval surroundings settled on and around her with a sense of timelessness and peace unlike anything she had ever experienced. Something elemental, it made her feel at one with the people of history during the last three millennia of which she had just been reading.

After the last zigzag, Allie saw the arched gate in the west curtain wall ahead of her. Two ancient cypress trees guarded the entrance—two soldiers on the alert—while large supporting buttresses jutted off to each side.

Looking at the walls of the castle up close, Allie noticed that it was well preserved. Even though its ramparts were crumbling in places, they were still serviceable. She could easily imagine knights and their ladies riding through the gate with their men-at-arms marching behind them, the prince's standard fluttering in the wind from the tallest towers.

"What do you think?" Stavros asked.

"It's beautiful," she said but didn't tell him her true thoughts. Knowing his distrust of fairy tales, she suspected that he wouldn't appreciate them.

"I thought you'd like it." He lightly touched her shoulder to guide her around to face what the castle had guarded for centuries. "But the view is the best part."

As she turned and her eyes registered the beauty of the 180-degree scene stretched out below and beyond, she gasped. She had expected to see the patchwork valley and the mountains surrounding it like a protective hoop, but what she hadn't anticipated was the Ionian Sea, shining like a crystal world of enchantment, to the glimmering west.

"I didn't know the sea was visible from here or that Kastro was so close to it." She reached out her hand, feeling as though she were a titan who, with just three or four steps, could cross the golden valley and wade into the waters that, even from this distance, were the famous blue of Greece.

"As a crow flies, Kastro is only about forty kilometers from the sea," Stavros explained. "It was for this"—he stretched out his arm to encompass the land and seascape before them—"that this fort was built here. Even invaders by ship could be detected early."

"Amazing," she whispered in awe, while absently lifting her braid off her neck to let the wind touch her skin.

"Are you hot?"

With a rueful smile, she let the French braid swing back into place. "Surely you jest? With all this arctic coolness?" she replied facetiously, holding out her hand to the hot wind. "You?" she questioned.

His eyes opened wide in an "of course" gesture as he motioned toward the castle. "That's why I've ordered air-conditioning for dinner." Walking toward the steps leading up to the huge portal, he waited for her to follow.

"Air-conditioning?" Allie moved toward him. "What's that?" She hadn't felt air-conditioning since leaving the States, and she certainly hadn't expected to find it in a deserted castle high above the village. But after trailing Stavros just three paces into the interior of the vaulted passageway, she understood. Within its deep walls, the temperature was at least ten degrees cooler, if not more. "It's wonderful!"

"Ancient and medieval man's answer to scorching days was to hide behind his thick castle walls."

"And we of the modern world think that we are the only ones with the advantage of air-conditioning."

"No," he returned, and Allie thought she detected an ironic note in his voice. "We've just forgotten how to build houses of thick stones with deep foundations on solid rock that protect us from more than just the elements of the earth," he declared, and his jaw muscles became as tight as a bowstring.

Allie suspected that he was speaking figuratively and was referring to much more than just the physical home. The verses from the sixth chapter of the Gospel of Luke came to her mind. She spoke them without hesitancy.

"It has been well recorded that a very wise Man once said, 'I will show you what he is like who comes to me and hears my words and puts them into practice. He is like a man building a house, who dug down deep and laid the foundation on rock. When a flood came, the torrent struck that house but could not shake it, because it was well built.' " She paused.

"Jesus' words," Stavros murmured.

She nodded, somewhat taken back that he recognized them. But it was a pleasant surprise.

"Please continue."

Feeling as if something very important was happening, she did. "'But the one who hears my words and does not put them into practice is like a man who built a house on the ground without a foundation. The moment the torrent struck that house, it collapsed and its destruction was complete.'"

Only the sounds of the natural world around them—the swallows playing in the evening sky, the trees, bushes, and dust of the earth being moved by the wind, bees buzzing—could be heard for a few moments as the words of the Lord settled between them.

"I am not an infidel, Allie." His voice was deep, but with a quality Allie could only describe as resigned sadness. "I believe that Jesus Christ is God's Son and that He came from heaven to earth to set all people free from sin so that we might have everlasting life."

Her soul sang to hear his declaration, even as she asked, "But even still, you don't trust Him to care for you here and now, do you?"

He rubbed his hand over his face and sighed, the deep, troubled sound of a man who had walked too long along life's rough paths alone. She wasn't surprised when he changed the subject. "How about if we eat?" he asked.

Allie smiled her agreement as she watched him pull the backpack from his shoulder. Knowing that he did believe in the redemptive work of Jesus was like learning that the vital signs of life were still present in a person who suffered from a serious illness. She was beginning to have an idea of what she was dealing with in him. She only hoped that before this night was over, she would learn more.

For Stavros Andreas was becoming more and more special to her.

***

Feed her he did.

But much, much more.

Stavros asked her to wait outside the castle entrance, beyond the supporting buttresses, while he set up the meal. When he called her in, he had transformed the entrance area into a hall fit for a king. Medieval tapestries hung upon the old walls, flickering sconces cast friendly shadows, and Allie thought that Emperor Alexius Comnenus himself might come riding in to join them.

Awed, she took in the lace tablecloth, the sterling silverware, and the hand-dipped candle of softest violet, lit beneath an antique crystal globe. She looked up at him. "Stavros, this is unbelievable." *And he claims not to believe in fairy tales!*

He smiled and pulled out one of the two chairs for her to be seated. "Since there aren't any fine restaurants in the vicinity of Kastro, I've had to learn how to improvise."

She laughed, but only to hide the unexpected stab of jealousy. "Oh? Do you bring many women up here?" she asked, slanting her eyes over at him as he took the other chair.

"You're the first."

She was confused. "Then…?"

"Jeannie. I bring Jeannie up here at least once a month," he explained, and Allie's lips turned up at the corners, both in unexpected relief and in happiness for the girl who had such a caring and doting father. "She loves it." He indicated the table. "The lace, the crystal, all of it. I keep a lot of stuff—table, chairs, lamp, plates, glasses—here permanently."

Allie looked at the items in alarm. He was talking about crystal and sterling, not glass and plastic. "People don't steal them?"

"Crime in Greece is very low—probably the lowest in Europe. Here in Kastro it's practically nonexistent."

"Except if there's a feud?" she suggested wryly.

He lifted his brows in sad agreement. Then, leaving that subject behind—something she was happy to do, too—he raised his glass. "To friendship," he said and smiled, a slow and giving one.

Lifting her long-stem glass, she knew that it was a pledge more than a toast—one she wouldn't argue with. She lightly touched the rim of her glass to his and accepted what he was offering with a joyful heart. "To friendship," she agreed before taking a sip of the refreshing liquid.

"Tell me," she asked after a quiet moment of harmonious reflection. "Martha mentioned that you moved here from Washington, D.C., three years ago. What were you doing when you lived there? Teaching?"

He reached over to the stone bench beside the table for a food container. "Yes. Medieval literature."

"What?" That was the last thing she had expected him to say.

"I'm a professor of medieval literature."

"A professor?" She had always known that there was more to this man than what he presented.

He nodded, and she asked, "Where did you teach?"

"Georgetown University."

She took a sip of water, then said, "I'm impressed."

"What I do here in Kastro is of far more lasting importance. Nothing is more wonderful than having the privilege of helping form young minds."

"Oh, I agree," she was hasty to assure him. "But having university qualifications makes you of greater worth to those budding brains simply because you know more. Tell me, what do you most enjoy about teaching kids?"

"That they are so honest. They tell it like it really is, like they see it. The world and everything to do with it."

She rubbed the stem of her crystal glass between her forefinger and thumb. "I've found that to be true when dealing with children in medicine, too. They want to know what I'm doing when I examine them. Why? Will it hurt? Everything. Even the diagnosis."

"And do you tell them?"

"If I can."

"Meaning?"

"You've probably discovered in teaching the same thing that I have in practicing family medicine—that often dealing with the parents is the most difficult part of the job."

He smiled in agreement. "How true."

The remainder of the meal passed with the same sort of companionable conversation.

A little later they sat on the steps of the castle, enjoying both a bowl of grapes and the view. The sun-ripened fruit tasted so fresh that Allie felt as though she could taste the sun in them, while the view was panoramic and alive with activity. She could almost envision Thumbelina riding on the back of a swallow that dipped in the breeze close to them. Without thinking, she spoke her thoughts. "All this—the meal, the view, the castle—it's truly like a fairy tale."

"This castle was anything but part of a fairy tale, Allie," he immediately cast back.

She didn't want to have another disagreement with him— especially during this very special evening. Holding up her hands in a conciliatory fashion, she said, "I didn't mean to imply—"

"Do you know the amount of blood that has been spilled right here where you now sit munching on your grapes so charmed by the view? Hundreds, thousands, of people have lost their lives," he said. "No, Allie, this land was too wealthy, too strategically located to be left to the fairy tales."

She regarded him steadily for a moment, angered that he had intentionally misunderstood her. "Oh yes, I forgot," she said sarcastically. "You don't like fairy tales, do you? Not even for children."

"Particularly not for children."

"Why, Stavros? Why are you such a pessimist that you can't let a little whimsy into your life? Into your daughter's life?"

"I'm not a pessimist, Allie. As I told you last night, I'm a realist. And my daughter is fine without idealistic stories to create unrealistic expectations within her little head."

"So you think you are being a realist by ignoring the lovely, the enchanting, the fanciful things in life? You think by ignoring them you can prevent hurt and pain in your life, in your daughter's life?"

"No," he ground out. "But I do believe that unrealistic expectations can be avoided that way. I don't believe in happily-ever-afters."

Allie sucked in her breath. "That's sad, very sad. Happily-ever-afters, those which have God in the equation," she qualified, "do exist, Stavros."

He regarded her for a moment. "Tell me, Allie Alexander, what is your idea of a happily-ever-after?" he asked but immediately held up his hand to stop her answer. "No, wait. I know. It's to marry the handsome, modern-day prince"—he opened his palms outward in a gesture that said he found it unbelievable—"and to live happily-ever-after, of course."

That was a bit too simple, but also, too close to reality. She lifted her chin. "And why not?"

"First and foremost, because you're a career woman."

She blinked. Had she missed something, a non sequitur, along the line? "What?"

"You're a professional," he repeated, as if that clarified everything.

"So?"

"You're married to your work."

She blinked again. "I am not!"

"Oh, come on, Allie. You just told me you don't even know how to cook," he said, referring to part of their mealtime conversation.

"So what you're saying is, one has to know how to cook in order to live the happily-ever-after life?"

He made a disgusted sound. "What I'm saying is I don't believe that professional women can have it all. They can't have a family and their profession. It doesn't work. Somebody always pays. The children, the woman, or the man." He paused. "Somebody."

Allie looked at him as a physician studying a patient. What she saw was pain deep in his eyes, pain that must often plague him. She had seen the same look in desperately ill people many times before. Consequently, she didn't get angry. What she did was get personal. "Tell me, Stavros. What exactly did your wife do to you to make you hurt so badly?"

As if someone had struck him, he flinched, and tears sprang into her eyes at the raw ache that filled his face. She moved her hand up between them and spoke softly, her bubble of self-righteous directness now popped. "I'm sorry. I had no right—"

"No," he waved her apology aside. The question had changed his demeanor, too. He spoke softly, no longer antagonistically. "No. Actually"—he paused and gave her a wry smile—"I want to tell you." He paused again. "I've never told anyone but my mother and Papouli what I am about to tell you but—"

"Stavros—"

"I want to tell you," he repeated, and nodding, she waited. "My wife—" He rubbed his hand over his eyes and took a deep breath. "She didn't want Jeannie. Not ever."

Allie couldn't help the gasp that came from her. She didn't know what she had expected him to say. Just—not that. Never that. But so much about the man she was coming to care a great deal about was explained by those words.

"When my wife," he continued, "found out she was pregnant, she wanted—" He stopped speaking and grimaced wryly. "Let's just say that until my wife was past a certain week in her pregnancy, I didn't let her out of my sight for fear of what harm she might do to our unborn child—my little baby—to Jeannie." He looked out over the valley, and Allie knew he wasn't seeing the view but that very difficult time instead.

Allie reached out and touched his upper arm. His biceps bulged beneath her hand. Such a strong man, and yet the strength that he had had to exert to protect his unborn child had been so much greater, a might, Allie was sure, from which he was still recovering. Allie didn't have to be told in any plainer words that his wife had wanted to abort Jeannie.

"Jeannie told me," she ventured softly after a moment, "that it was as if her mother was dead, even"—she paused—"when she was alive."

Like eagle eyes zooming in on the prey, his gaze swiveled back to hers, startling her. "Jeannie said that?" he asked in a strangled tone.

Perplexed by his piercing look, Allie shook her head in

confused question. "What does she normally say about her mother?"

"Nothing."

Her eyes widened in shock. "Nothing?"

"Absolutely nothing. To no one," he confirmed. "The topic of her mother is the only thing she never talks to me about. No matter what I do to try to get her to speak." He opened his hands before him, a parent's helpless gesture.

That Jeannie felt something very special toward Allie to have so honored her in speaking about her mother was obvious to both of them. She shrugged. "I don't know what to say."

"I do." Reaching out, he softly ran the back of his fingers against her jaw. His eyes darkened, and as she read only nice and wonderful things in their depths, things so different from what she had seen there just moments before, she breathed out a prayer of relief within her. "You are a godsend," he said, surprising her, but Allie could tell from the catch in his voice that he felt the same amazement over his own words.

He continued, "I believe, Allie Alexander, that you were actually sent by God—directed to come to Kastro even—to help my little girl and me. Her not talking about her mother has been a heavy burden for me to bear. Because I knew it was so unhealthy, I think it was the last thing that kept me from allowing my heart to trust God again. In spite of my wife, God has been good to us," he admitted. "I have known this intellectually for quite some time." He breathed out deeply. "My heart was just too hard and heavy to admit that which my mind's eye could see."

His lips slowly turned up at their corners, and Allie watched as the most remarkable smile spread across his face. It matched the smile in his eyes. "You are quite some physician, Dr.

Alexander. Not only does my little girl open up to you in a way she hasn't to anyone else, but"—he placed the palm of his hand over his chest—"I feel as though my heart, which has felt more like a heavy block of ice than a beating pump, is finally beginning to melt."

"Oh, Stavros." She covered his hand with hers. Then, twining their fingers together, she scooted closer and rested her head against his chest, against the beating of his heart. She closed her eyes as its steady sound filled her ear. "I hear it, Stavros. I feel it. It's warm, my darling. It's warm and strong."

He squeezed her closer to him and spoke into her hair. "Maybe in God sending you to Kastro and to me, I can finally start to believe that He really does care about me, about Jeannie."

"Oh, Stavros," Allie whispered and, sitting back a little, looked up at him. "He does. He really, really does."

"My life was just so perfect until"—he paused—"my wife became pregnant." A faraway look came into his eyes. "I never knew that she didn't want children."

"You never talked about having a family someday?" That seemed inconceivable to Allie. Her family had always talked— and prayed—about everything.

He took a deep breath and shook his head. "No. I just assumed that someday we would start a family. It wasn't an assumption my wife shared."

"Did your wife…I mean, did she believe in God?"

"That's the funny thing." He clicked his tongue against his cheek. "She did." He shrugged his shoulders. "I guess she got lost somewhere along the way." He looked at her as if he were trying to measure her. "You told me last night you would never have made it to Kastro if you hadn't lived your life God's way rather than your own. What did you mean?"

As if she had been doing it forever, she turned and leaned her back against him. She breathed in deeply of the pure air, while her eyes took in the surrounding beauty. The sun was riding low in the sky, highlighting the blue of the sea, while the earth was rejoicing in the rest a star-filled night would soon bring to it. Looking out over the world bathed in the setting sun and holding his arms close around her, she prayed for wisdom in answering.

"When I sit at a place like this, I feel so thankful to be alive and to know who it is that keeps me safely in His grip." She squeezed Stavros's hand. Then, turning her head to look up into his waiting eyes, she answered him directly. "My mother died when I was just a little girl, and even though I had the most wonderful father in the world and a brother who would have given me the moon itself had I asked him for it, I would not have been a happy girl if I hadn't been assured of my heavenly Father's love. There is only so much people can and should expect of their fellow humans. I learned at a very young age that people leave us—people we love and who love us. The only constant in life is God, as revealed by Jesus Christ. He is here with me now, just as he was in New York City and Athens, too.

If I had tried to live my life without that constant, I know that I never would have left what seemed like my secure world. I would have lived life my way rather than God's way. He directed me to go to Athens to continue my studies." She gave a shaky laugh as she remembered that time. "And believe me, that was no small decision. Just as He then directed me to Kastro."

Stavros shook his head. There was an amazed yet a respectful quality to his voice as he said, "I think what you have is a very mature working faith in God."

She smiled self-consciously. "That's what my brother, Alex, has always said. What about you, Stavros?"

He took a deep breath and confessed, "I've always believed in God. I never stopped believing, even when I felt He didn't care about Jeannie or me or all the rest of the hurting people in the world." He grimaced. "But I think that the measure of my faith went along with how well everything was working out in my life. When things went wrong—particularly when my wife didn't want our baby—I think I decided that God really didn't care. My faith became as weak as my life, when just the opposite should have happened." He shook his head. "I don't know. Maybe I was an idealist, one who felt as though my happily-ever-after life was ripped wrongly away from me when my wife didn't want the baby I thought our love had conceived. Perhaps I was even one, as you said, whose principles were shattered—shattered into a million pieces."

"To be an idealist is not something bad, Stavros. It's only when you believe in your ideals more than you do God, or when you rely on your belief of how everything should be rather than on your faith in God to work all things out for your good, that it's not advantageous."

He nodded. "I'll concede that. It's very shocking, though, when things don't work out as one plans."

"So be a hopeful realist, like me."

"Hopeful realist." He seemed to taste the expression. "I like that." Then, standing, he pulled her up with him, effectively but nicely ending their discussion as he had on so many other occasions. Allie didn't mind. She had learned so much about him during the last few minutes, really important things that had brought them very close.

"Come. It's getting dark. I'd better direct you down the path before it's too dark to see."

"Path," Allie murmured the word she found key to his sentence—to their conversation—and recited a favorite verse from Psalm 119. "'Your word is a lamp to my feet and a light for my path.'"

He paused, and the smile he gave her in the waning light of the day made her wonder if he might just be the knight—the Christian knight—she had been dreaming about her whole life. "You're quite a physician, Allie Alexander," he said, repeating the praise he had given her earlier.

"Oh, but it is the Great Physician who is working in your heart, Stavros Andreas. Not I."

He clicked his tongue against his cheek as they walked together down the path to the village, and she heard him whisper, "I think, maybe, both of you are."

Chapter 16—Back Woodsman

The days that followed were, on a personal level, some of the most wonderful Allie had ever experienced. That she and Stavros had been brought together by God, and that their growing feelings had been ordained by Him, was something of which they were both becoming certain. When Allie wasn't at her clinic, she was with Stavros and Jeannie at their apartment, or they were with her at her apartment, or the three of them were visiting with Papouli and Martha, or they were walking the countryside around Kastro, hand in hand. It was as Jeannie had proclaimed when the three of them had returned home from Papouli's together on Allie's first night in Kastro—it was as if they were a family.

But the clinic was still a problem.

It wasn't that things weren't going well; rather, things weren't going. Period.

She had no patients. Not even the elderly came to have their blood pressure taken, something Allie had been told was a favorite pastime for the senior citizens of the village. That Drakopoulos had instigated a boycott on the clinic was obvious.

Allie thought about threatening the Men's Club with going to the Department of Health again, as she had after the office had been vandalized. But after much prayer, she knew God wanted her to trust Him and to leave the situation in His capable hands. Casting all her anxieties on Him, she put on the virtue of patience and waited.

Allie didn't mind for herself. She used the free time to acquaint herself with the people she was to serve through the numerous and meticulous medical ledgers her predecessor had left behind. But she did mind for Sophia.

Because of Sophia's tenuous position—her husband being Tasos Drakopoulos's brother—the woman didn't come to the office as Allie had asked her, nor did she feel comfortable enough to allow Allie to examine her at her home. This disturbed Allie. Her professional intuition warned her that Sophia and her baby might just become real victims of this feud.

On the fourth day the clinic was open, Allie decided that if the people of the area wouldn't come to her, she would go to them. She read in the medical records about a family of four children who lived up on the mountain with their father and had not received their current inoculations. She decided to pay the family a visit. When she leaned from Stavros why the family lived all alone up on the mountain, her heart went out to them.

The man's wife had died in childbirth three years earlier. Angry at the so-called civilized world, which had not been able to save his wife and baby, Petros Petropoulos had taken his four children and returned to his ancestral home to live an extremely basic life. When Stavros went on to tell her that Petropoulos was in fact the man who had disembarked from the bus with the chickens on the day she arrived, Allie was further intrigued. She couldn't help but think of Johanna Spyri's beloved heroine, Heidi, who had lived high on a mountain with her grandfather.

When Stavros offered to take her to the family on his horse, her house call turned into a very romantic trip up the mountain. Especially when Papouli, ever the matchmaker, prompted Jeannie to stay behind with Martha. They were going to make *hilopitas*—or "thousand pastas"—homemade pasta cut into a thousand little squares.

"Well, Dr. Alexander," Stavros said, as he came to stand

before Allie when his daughter and the priest left the clinic. "It seems as though we can spend some quality time alone this morning." He motioned in the direction where the old priest's laughter and the little girl's chatter could still be heard as they made their way up the village road toward Papouli's home. "I love my daughter." He rubbed the back of his hand against Allie's cheek, and she watched as his dimples, a sure sign that he was happy and content, deepened around his mouth. "But I am glad to be alone with the woman I am coming to love, too."

"Love?" Allie whispered hesitantly. She was glad he had been the first to mention what was obviously in the air between them, but at the same time, she just wasn't sure she could make such a declaration with her job in Kastro still so tenuous.

He nodded, then placing his finger against her lips and seeming to read her mind, he said, "Let's get your situation here settled." Leaning toward her, he placed a feather-soft kiss upon her lips. "Then we have to talk."

"Talk?" she repeated, her heart giving a little flutter.

"Hmm…but first your position here has to be set." He smiled sheepishly, as they both remembered how difficult he had made her stay in the beginning. "I understand now how important it is to you—and to the health of the people in this rural location—and I will not do anything—anything else, that is—to make it any harder for you than it already is."

"Thank you, Stavros," she said. "You know, with your support, I feel as though I can do almost anything."

She had always thought that she really needed only God in her life. Now, after having come to have such strong feelings for Stavros, she understood that to have both God and the love of a man of faith—and Stavros was now, indeed, just that—was ideal. But then again, hadn't God Himself ordained that man and woman should pass through life together? No wonder the joy she felt in having Stavros by her side was so perfect.

He wrapped his arms around her and pulled her near him. She reveled in the feel of having him so close, both physically and emotionally. "You can do anything, my love," he whispered in her ear. "You can."

***

"There. Now that didn't hurt much, did it?" Allie asked two hours later of the wobbly-lipped little boy named Vassili as she rubbed the spot on his hip where she had just inoculated him.

"That nail I stepped on yesterday hurt a whole lot more," the boy assured her, trying his best not to let tears slip from his eyes.

Concerned, Allie asked, "What nail, *agori mou*—my boy?"

The boy lifted his bare foot and showed her the makeshift bandage that covered the puncture.

"I washed it and put iodine on it, Yatrinna, " sixteen-year-old Maria explained, holding her youngest sibling's hand. Allie smiled at the sweet girl. She felt sorry for Maria. It was as if childhood had totally passed the girl by. Allie wished she could somehow convince the children's father to move back down to the village where they might have some help.

When she turned back to the boy's foot and removed the bandage, though, Allie had to use all her bedside manners not to flinch at the angry cut she found there. It was red and infected in spite of Maria's ministrations. "You did a good job, Maria." Allie knew the girl had done all that could be done under such primitive conditions, but to the boy she asked, "Do you still have the nail?"

"Sure do! I saved it!" The boy answered as Allie suspected he would. From both her brother and Dale, Allie knew that boys liked saving things like nails. Especially nails they had stepped on. "It's in my jar."

"I'll get it," Stephanos, the oldest boy, who was a year younger than Maria, offered, and walking over to the bed on the other side of the large, one-room house, he pulled a ceramic jar out from under it and brought it to his younger brother.

The boy rummaged through his treasures before presenting the nail to Allie as if it were a trophy.

She couldn't help widening her eyes. It was the rustiest, most jagged piece of metal she had ever seen. Although it had probably been a nail at one time, it hardly looked like one anymore. She thought it was probably left over from some Byzantine building. "Hmm, I guess that hurt a bit."

"A lot," the boy corrected her.

"Well, I'm afraid that you are going to have to have another shot."

"But why?" His lip wobbled again.

Talking on his level, she answered, "To make sure that rusty ol' nail doesn't make you sick."

"Oh." That seemed to calm him down. "I don't wanna be sick."

Allie ruffled his nearly blond hair, which, she had noticed with some surprise, was very clean. All the Petropoulos children were clean, as was their rustic but very quaint home. "You won't be."

But as she prepared the injection, she glanced up at Stavros. They both knew that if she hadn't come today the little boy might have become very ill with tetanus. She glanced over at Kyrios Petropoulos. She was surprised to realize he seemed to know it, as well.

He nodded at her, but in an enigmatic way, as if he had just made a big decision. "When you're finished here, Yatrinna, please come out and we'll talk." Motioning for Stavros to precede him, the two men walked out the door.

Allie watched them go before turning back to her job. She liked Petros Petropoulos. When he wasn't holding squiggling, squawking chickens, as he had been that day on the bus, he was a very calm, articulate man. He remembered her and had been amazed when she rode up with Stavros. He was more amazed still when he found out she was Kastro's new doctor. Not because she was a woman, but because she cared enough about his children to ride all the way up the mountain to check on them.

After the children were all taken care of, she left them with one of the many puzzles she had brought for the younger patients in the village and went out to join the men. They were sitting at a table made from the trunk of a big oak tree with matching stools from the same tree's branches. Expertly shellacked, it was a natural and beautiful patio set, and Allie knew that people in New York would have gladly paid top dollar for it.

"How's the boy?" Petropoulos asked quickly, exhibiting all the concern a doctor could want in a patient's parent.

"He'll be fine. I've left an ointment and some tablets for him to take." She paused. "That nail was very rusty. Didn't you think he might need a tetanus shot?"

"I only got back this morning. I was up in the pine forest checking on my trees. The children told me about it. I hadn't seen the nail. I was as shocked as you."

Allie wondered how he would have felt had his child

184

suddenly and needlessly developed tetanus. She said, "Kyrios Petropoulos, you're a long way from civilization and help if you ever needed it. Why don't you move the children back down to the village? I'm sure someone could be found to help with the housework, and your children could go to school." Allie had already discovered that all of the children were extremely bright.

"I think you're right," Petros answered without even pausing.

Stavros turned his head toward him as quick as a whiplash. "What?"

Petros smiled. "I said, I think the doctor is right."

"But I've been trying for the last two years to get you to move off this mountain and back down to the village."

"Yatrinna!" Vassili called out. "We finished the puzzle. Do you want to see it?"

Allie flashed Stavros an amused smile before she stretched out her legs and rose from her seat. She could tell he was not only amazed by his friend's answer but flabbergasted. She bit her lip to keep from laughing at his expression and, turning to Petros, said, "I'm glad you're going to move to the village. I'm looking forward to seeing a lot more of your children—and I don't mean only for medical reasons," she qualified before excusing herself and returning to the well-behaved siblings.

"*Einai koukla,*" Petros said of Allie just as he had that day at the bus stop.

Stavros stiffened. "Is that the reason you're moving back down? You're interested in the doctor?"

"Don't be ridiculous, friend. You and she are meant to be together just as my Emily and I were."

Stavros was surprised that Petros had not only so quickly noticed but said something about it. The woodsman was a man of few words, giving each one he spoke more weight. "Then why are you suddenly coming down off this mountain?"

"Because I have a good enough reason to move now." Petros nodded toward the door Allie had just walked though. "That doctor will do everything humanly possible to make sure no more of my babies die."

"But Kastro has had other doctors. Don't you think they would have, too?"

Petros made a disgusted noise. "They never even cared enough to come looking for us," he spat out, and Stavros knew that he spoke the truth. Both of the other two physicians were eager to leave Kastro. They had only wanted to serve their required year and get out, definitely not anything above and beyond the call of duty. Allie Alexander, they weren't.

Stavros frowned. He wondered why he hadn't thought of that before. Allie was the only doctor who had come to Kastro because she *wanted* to and not because of governmental requirements. And everyone, including him, had made life difficult for her.

***

A little while later, clip-clopping down the mountain on their return trip to Kastro with Allie seated before him on Charger, Stavros kissed the sensitive part of her neck where her braid—now just one long band of beautifully twisted hair—fell. "Thank you, darling Allie."

The saddle creaked as she squirmed around and looked up at him in question. "For what?"

"For coming to Kastro and being instrumental in saving two recluses—Petros and me."

She put her hand up to his face. "Oh, my darling, don't you know you have done the same for me?"

Stavros was glad that Charger knew the way back to Kastro. He only had eyes for the beautiful woman he held tightly in his arms.

At Allie's request, Stavros—and Charger—left her at the clinic. She had some paperwork to complete plus she wanted to be available during the evening hours in case someone decided they needed a doctor more than they needed to be a part of a silly feud. After two hours, when still no one came, she closed up and headed for home, deciding to stop at Sophia's shop on the pretense of needing something.

Pushing through the beads, Allie expected to see Sophia in her usual place behind the carved counter. She wasn't there; rather, she was sitting on a hardback café chair with her head resting against the wall and her eyes closed. Allie walked quietly up to her and placed her hand against her forehead. She became alarmed when she felt how clammy the woman was.

Sophia's eyes fluttered opened. When she saw Allie, she smiled.

"Yatrinna." Her voice was even softer than normal, and slowly, wearily, like a very old woman, her hand reached up to take Allie's. Allie took the chance to feel for her pulse. She was relieved to find it normal.

"Sophia, you're exhausted. What are you doing here?"

"Yiannie, my husband, had to check on something in the fields—the vines—I didn't want to shut the shop."

"Let me put you to bed and examine you. Please, Sophia. I'm worried about you—"

"There's no need." A harsh voice spoke from behind, and Allie didn't need to turn around to know to whom it belonged.

Allie would have known the Wicked Witch of the West, the evil Elani Drakopoulos, anywhere. "My relative doesn't need a stranger looking after her," she continued and grabbed Sophia's hand away from Allie.

"Kyria Drakopoulos, your relative is a very pregnant woman who is utterly exhausted. She should be in bed, preferably a hospital bed, where she can have tests performed."

The beads from the back of the house rustled, and they all looked up as a man whom Allie assumed to be Sophia's husband entered. He was of medium to short height, and Allie thought him a man of medium to short personality, as well, for allowing his wife's health, and that of his unborn child's, to be put in danger because of some archaic feud.

"Elani? Sophia?" He glanced at Allie in question, and she extended her hand. He took it. Allie held it for a moment. She wasn't surprised to find his grasp extremely weak.

"Kyrios Drakopoulos, I'm Dr. Alexander. I strongly suggest that your wife be taken down to the hospital and given complete rest, as well as tests."

"Don't be ridiculous," Elani cackled. "She's fine. Just a little tired from a day of making hilopitas. "

Allie turned to Sophia aghast. "Hilopitas!" she exclaimed. Ordinarily, making the pasta wasn't a very difficult task for village women. But a full day of mixing dough, rolling it out into paper thin sheets, cutting it into a thousand tiny pieces, then putting it in the sun to dry was definitely something Sophia shouldn't have been doing. "Sophia, that's too much for you in your condition."

"It's okay," Sophia whispered, and Allie noticed that speaking seemed too much for her now.

Allie turned to her husband. "I strongly suggest your wife

be taken down to the hospital—"

"No," Elani forcefully interrupted. "She doesn't need a hospital. Just her bed."

Ignoring the other woman's outburst, Allie continued to speak to Sophia's husband. "Kyrios Drakopoulos, I think that your wife is suffering from a mild case of heat exhaustion. She needs care."

Indecision weighed heavily on the man's shoulders. He was definitely a weak man who had probably been in his brother's shadow all his life. But for a moment, Allie thought she saw something like agreement flicker through his eyes. But his sister-in-law moved, making her position clear.

"I'll put Sophia to bed now," she said, expertly taking charge, and Allie watched in amazement as Sophia's husband shrugged his shoulders in compliance—something he had probably done a thousand times before.

Allie felt defeated. "Sophia?" She appealed to the exhausted woman.

"I'll—be—fine, Yatrinna, " she whispered as she allowed her sister-in-law to guide her toward the back area.

With those words Allie knew there was nothing more she could do. Feeling as though she had been slapped in the face, she returned in her most professional tone, "Drink plenty of cool drinks and don't hesitate to call me if you need anything." Turning, she walked out the shop door.

But all the way up the cobbled streets toward home, Allie was mad, so mad she was sure steam could be seen coming from her ears. She didn't understand how people could be so careless with their health, with the health of their unborn children. What these people needed wasn't a doctor but a good swift kick in the rear end.

She only hoped that dear Sophia wouldn't be the one to get kicked.

But at the moment Allie couldn't even understand how the shopkeeper could be so silly as to make hilopitas. True, it hadn't been over 110 degrees as on the previous days, but it had still reached well up into the nineties. Hot. Too hot for a woman who was at least forty years old and about to have a baby for the first time to be making her winter supply of pasta.

As Allie stomped her way into the garden of her house, she decided that dealing with the mentality of these villagers was much more difficult than tackling their diseases. She walked toward the fountain in the garden. Not having running water in her house to have a bath made it almost unbearable. Allie knew she was behaving unreasonably, but when the broad leaf of the banana tree reached out and slapped her arm as she stormed passed it, she balled up her fist and swung into the leaf. Not once, not twice, not three times, but more, and she probably wouldn't have stopped swinging if an iron grip hadn't taken hold of her arm from behind and halted her.

"Allie!" Stavros called out. "Have you gone mad?"

"No!" She whirled around to face him, forcing him to let go of her. "I haven't gone mad, but I am mad. Mad, mad, mad!" she yelled out. "Sophia could die, or the baby, or they both could, and nobody cares because of this stupid feud—one whose origin nobody can even remember. Not even Papouli remembers. It's getting to be a tedious excuse."

With extreme gentleness he pulled her close to him, and the fight left her like air from a balloon. She leaned against him, and relief settled around her like a cloud.

She needed him.

She needed his arms.

She needed just to be held.

After so long, so many years of standing like a tall cypress tree at guard, Allie needed to lean like a weeping willow. And she needed this man to bend toward, to depend upon.

Stavros ran his hand across her back, a caring gesture.

She squeezed her arms tighter around his neck, a needing gesture.

He responded by holding her closer and by raining little kisses of tenderness on the top of her head, down her cheek, on her throat.

Turning her head, she sought out his lips.

They were like the wonderful heat of the hot sand after staying in the cold sea too long. They warmed her soul, her spirit, and she knew that with this man she wanted the happily-ever-after to be theirs.

"Stavros…," she whispered against his mouth.

Gingerly, with infinite care, while keeping her in the circle of his arms, he stepped back. "Tell me what happened."

She told him. "Sophia isn't taking care of herself, and whenever I start to make headway with her, Elani Drakopoulos always seems to appear and tells her how she doesn't need me." She leaned her head wearily against his shoulder. "I'm just so worried about her."

Stavros reached beneath her braid and started kneading the tension that was as thick as a gnarled olive tree branch out of her neck. "I know…darling…I know."

Her eyes closed as she luxuriated in the magic his fingers were working on her neck. "Mmm…that feels so good."

"Close your eyes—"

"Well, well," Tasos Drakopoulos's nasally voice droned out from his place next to the open garden gate. "What have we here?"

Allie's muscles bunched as she almost reflexively stepped apart from Stavros. But with a slight pressure, he held her fast. They hadn't been doing anything wrong.

"Drakopoulos." Stavros greeted the other man.

"Thaskalos." Drakopoulos called Stavros by the title of teacher, just as the children and most of the parents in the village did.

"Why don't you let the doctor examine Sophia?" Stavros asked directly.

"That's not up to me." Drakopoulos spoke as if he were totally innocent. "That's up to Sophia."

"We both know that's not so."

"Do we?" the nasally voice returned.

Allie addressed him, the fire of injustice in her voice. "If she dies, or her baby does, I'll hold you and your wife responsible," she warned and was sure she didn't miss the flash of concern that went through his narrow eyes. But it passed, leaving only the latent anger of before.

"Sophia and her baby will be fine," he declared and returned to his favorite pastime, making her life miserable. "What I'm certain about, though, is that everyone is going to be very interested in learning how you two spend your days—and your nights," he snickered, and Allie and Stavros stood together as they watched him walk away.

"What an awful man," Allie said between gritted teeth.

"Be prepared for some bad days."

"Worse than the ones I've had?"

He slanted his gaze down to hers. "He just found us in one another's arms."

"But we haven't done anything," she protested.

"I know." A muscle jumped in his jaw. He motioned toward the house. "But we live here together. People will believe what they want to believe."

Allie sighed and leaned her head against his shoulder. She knew he was right. Hadn't she gone through this once before with the soccer player? But this time Stavros and Jeannie were involved, two of the dearest people in the world to her.

She wouldn't let them get hurt.

She closed her eyes and knew that not for anything would she allow that.

Chapter 17—Accusations & Miracles

It wasn't quite as hot in the morning as it was the previous day, but it was windless, and Allie soon learned that a scorcher in Kastro without the hot wind was worse than one with it.

She wanted—no, needed—a bath. She had opted for sponge baths since her second evening in the village, not wanting the chore of carrying bucket after bucket of water up the stairs. This morning, however, nothing would do except for full immersion in the elegant tub.

Donning a pair of shorts and T-shirt, she pushed the IN USE sign under Stavros's door, then walked down to the faucet in the garden and proceeded to fill the four metal buckets that sat ready by its side. Papouli walked into the garden, and Allie happily greeted him, but from the somber look on his face she knew that something was wrong.

"Is it Sophia? The baby?" she asked, shutting off the spigot in anticipation of having to run quickly down to Sophia's house.

Papouli held up his hand. "No, it's not a medical emergency."

"Then what—?"

Stavros opened his door and looked down on them from the veranda. "Papouli?"

"I need to speak with both of you," the older man said, looking up at him.

Leaving his door open, Stavros immediately came down and stood beside Allie. "What is it?"

Papouli got right to the point. "Some ugly things are being said"—he paused and looked over the rim of his glasses from one to the other—"about the two of you."

"Drakopoulos." Stavros spoke the man's name almost as if it were an epithet, and Papouli nodded.

"He's sitting in the *kafenion* telling everyone that you two"— the wise old man's eyes went questioningly from one to the other—"have been behaving improperly."

"That's not true, Papouli." Stavros answered the question in the priest's eyes without hesitation.

"I didn't think so," the old priest said, but Allie could tell from the way his shoulders relaxed that he was relieved. He might be a priest, but he was also a man and understood about temptation.

She gently laid her hand upon his arm. "Papouli, we aren't going to lie to you. As you might have suspected, Stavros and I are very attracted to one another. But we haven't done anything that would compromise our working in this village. Nothing which you—or God—would disapprove of."

That's all Papouli needed to hear. He was satisfied. "Thank you, Yatrinna. You didn't have to tell me this."

"You didn't have to warn us."

"Exactly what's being said?" Stavros asked, and Allie could tell that the priest didn't want to answer.

"Please, Papouli," Allie prompted, and the older man nodded.

"They're calling for Stavros's immediate resignation as teacher because he's 'carrying on' with you, the village doctor."

"What?"

"You've got to be kidding!"

"I'm afraid not," Papouli said, answering their disbelief.

"But this is my home. I love these kids, and they're all doing so well. Last year all the high school students who took the test for the university were admitted." Allie could hear the pain beneath Stavros's words, and she was amazed he really thought that made a difference to people like Drakopoulos. Unless Drakopoulos had a drastic change of heart, she doubted he would ever think of anyone over his own selfish desires.

But Allie also recognized that it was because of her and her insistence on living in Stavros's house that she had not only shaken, but was about to topple, the secure world Stavros had painstakingly built for his daughter and himself. She wasn't sure his newly reestablished faith would be able to withstand it.

"I'll take care of it," she said, and forgetting all about her bath, she left the pails of water where they were and pushed passed Stavros toward the stairs.

He reached out for her hand. Hesitantly, she turned to him. The pain in his eyes over the priest's revelation was countered by something good, something strong. She was amazed when she realized that it was a sense of togetherness. "We'll take care of it," he corrected her.

She appreciated his offer—loved it—but shook her head. "No, Stavros. It's not your problem."

"Not my problem?" he shot out questioningly. "How do you figure that?"

She gently squeezed his hand to stop further protest. "Don't you see, my love, they are just trying to get to me through you." *And they have*, a little voice whispered within her. They finally attacked her where she was vulnerable. Stavros and Jeannie. She could withstand attacks against herself, but not against those she loved. And she loved the Andreas family very much. "I'll handle it," she repeated with conviction.

"And just how do you plan on 'handling' it?" he asked through a jaw that had suddenly gone tight.

She smiled down at her shorts and T-shirt. "I'm going to go dress—extremely professionally," she qualified and lifted her brows at the amused look that jumped into his eyes. It felt so nice to be able to say something like that to him now and not to receive a negative response. After much talk he understood that his wife's professionalism had been to the extreme and that there were many women who could successfully juggle a career and a happy home life. The key was wanting to and knowing who to rely on to make it work. "Then, I'm going to pay the men at the Men's Club a little visit." Giving his hand another little squeeze, an encouraging one this time, she let go and, swiveling around, started running up the stairs.

Stavros followed close on her heels. "Allie. I want to come with you."

She spun around. Letting her eyes shine at with how cherished his words made her feel, she explained however why having him by her side at this time wouldn't work. "Thank you, my love, for wanting to, but don't you see? It's my profession that is being attacked, and because of this, it's something I must handle on my own and in my own way." She gave a light chuckle, then looked between the two men. "Which will actually be—"

"Not alone, but with God and…in God's way," Stavros finished and returned her smile with one of admiration.

"Ah…" the wise old priest said. "If only more people knew that secret."

Allie's gaze moved to his. "But I will most gladly accept any prayers you both might like to put forth on my behalf."

"Done," Papouli said.

Nodding, Stavros copied the older man. "Absolutely," he whispered.

As Allie turned away, the admiration and love coming from Stavros's whole being gave her courage. Knowing she had the love and prayers of such a man not only on her side but by her side was a blessing, one she accepted with a thankful heart.

***

Dressed in a pale green suit of linen, Allie walked into the *kafenion*.

It was full of smirking little men that made Allie ashamed for the rest of the masculine gender. Sour-faced Dionysia—as usual the only woman in the room—gave a defiant tilt of her face before disappearing into the curtained-off back room.

Allie didn't care. She turned to the table where she knew Drakopoulos would be holding court.

He immediately spoke. "I told you the people would all be very interested in learning about what I saw last night," his nasally voice gloatingly informed her.

Allie wasn't even going to justify his statement with one of her own. Instead, she asked, "What is it that you want?"

"I want you to leave."

"Why? Do you think your son will come if I go?" she asked directly and knew that she had hit a sensitive cord when there was a general movement around the room. Even though everyone knew the reason for Drakopoulos's behavior, no one had spoken it.

Blood vessels popped in the man's red forehead, and Allie was sure that his blood pressure was up. "He should have been given this job. Not you," he sneered.

Allie shrugged her shoulders. "That had nothing to do with me. I applied for the position, and it was awarded to me. Maybe your son applied too late. Or maybe," she paused dramatically, "he didn't apply at all because he didn't want to live around you."

Drakopoulos jumped up. He towered over Allie. But she didn't let so much as a muscle move. "How dare you?"

"Dare I? It's you who is causing all the problems. I only want to do my job."

"And sleep with the schoolteacher," the man spat out. "Something easy to do with that central hall. How do we know what really goes on there night after night?"

"You don't. You can only think what your wicked little minds allow you to think." She wasn't going to defend herself to this mindless group. Papouli knew the truth. She did. And Stavros. That's all that mattered.

"Well, we've decided." He gestured at all the men in the room. "If you're not on the afternoon bus, the teacher will not be allowed to teach at our school this year."

"Yes, I've heard that."

"So."

"So that's how you got me here. Now tell me what it is that you want."

"I told you. I want you on the afternoon bus."

"Mr. Drakopoulos," Allie began quietly but firmly, "currently, everything is fine in your world—your wife is well, your friends." She waved her hand around the room. "But I wonder. How would you feel if I got on that bus and tomorrow or the next day your wife should fall ill, or a friend of yours should suffer a heart attack, or one of the children in the village should fall and need a doctor, and you know that you are responsible for my leaving and thus for the people you care about not having the help they need?"

"Another doctor will come—hopefully, my son."

Allie laughed, a sound that was like a lawyer's laugh of contempt. "Do you honestly think I would leave this village and not tell the Department of Health how I was threatened into leaving? And knowing the reason, do you honestly believe they will allow Kastro to retain control of the Rural Physician's Station for this area?"

"We'll tell them you were behaving improperly," he threatened, and although Allie felt that old tightening in her stomach over the false accusation, she didn't even let so much as her voice waver or her hand shake as she continued.

"I like Mr. Andreas. I like him very much," she admitted. "But we have never behaved in an improper manner."

That old evil smile, that smile that showed his gold teeth in the back of his mouth, stretched across his face. "But you don't have proof."

She had proof, the ultimate proof. But that was only her business and that of the man she eventually married—hopefully Stavros. "I tell you what we are going to do." She tapped her nails against the tabletop. "I'm going to pretend this episode never happened—write it off to the heat doing things to your brain—and I'm going to go to my office right now, and if anyone has a need, they can find me there during office hours or at my home after hours. I hope no one needs my skills," her eyes touched on individual ones in the room, "because that will mean that all in this village—your wives, your children, your mothers, your fathers—are well. But I will be available if I am needed, and I will help everyone to the best of my—"

"Dionysia! Dionysia!" A woman ran into the café, and everyone turned to her.

Dionysia appeared instantly from behind the curtain where

she had obviously been listening to what was going on. "What is it?" she rasped out.

"It's Sophia. She's collapsed!"

"Oh, dear Lord!" Allie breathed out and went over to the other woman, one whom Allie recognized as having helped clean the clinic after it had been vandalized. "Where is she?"

The woman glanced over Allie's shoulder at Tasos. He was scowling, but Allie was relieved to see that the woman didn't seem to care. This was an emergency, and in emergencies nothing mattered except the person in need—definitely not the opinion of Tasos Drakopoulos. "In front of her store. She'd been hanging clothes out, walked into the street, and fainted."

But Allie heard the tail end as she ran out the door. Moments later, she tore into the clinic, thankful that it was located so close to Sophia's home. Grabbing her medical bag and miniature ICU case, she ran up to Sophia's house. A crowd of people had gathered around the spot where Sophia was lying in the road.

"Let me through!" Allie shouted. The crowd parted, and Allie was further appalled when she saw that hardly anything was being done for the unconscious woman. Elani Drakopoulos was uselessly fanning Sophia's face. When she saw Allie, she looked up and snarled like a dog. "We don't need you."

Ignoring her, Allie set her bags down, reached for Sophia's pulse, and grimaced. It was disturbed, her skin was hot, and she wasn't sweating. "Heatstroke," she murmured and took precious seconds to speak to Sophia's husband, who was hovering over his wife impotently. "If you don't let me treat your wife now, she is going to die and your baby, too."

Before Allie's very eyes, she watched a weak man turn into a strong one.

"She's just trying to scare you!" Elani Drakopoulos shouted, but Sophia's husband pushed her back and, like a lead dog protecting his territory, snapped at the people. "We will do exactly as the doctor says."

That was all Allie needed to hear. She got to work. "Let's get her inside where it's cool," she instructed, and several men immediately lifted Sophia and carried her to the room behind the store, where a bed was located. "I need ice, lots of ice, and electric fans," Allie told them, and they quickly scurried away to comply. While she was setting up an IV, she instructed the women, "Get her clothes off her and get wet towels onto her. She's burning up, and we've got to get her fever down," she informed them while inserting the needle into Sophia's hand.

"Here's a fan." One of the men returned, and Allie instructed him to get it blowing directly onto Sophia. Within moments, two more fans were in place, and cool towels covered Sophia's body. Allie took her temperature and shook her head.

"What is it?" she heard a deep, gravelly voice ask, and she looked up into Papouli's concerned eyes.

"One hundred and six degrees."

"Is there anything I can do?"

"Pray."

Papouli smiled. "I'm good at that."

"Yatrinna," Mr. Drakopoulos hesitantly asked. "Is...is she going to be okay?"

"I'm going to do everything I can to make sure that she is."

"But she's still unconscious."

Allie nodded as she placed her fetal stethoscope up against Sophia's bulging tummy. "But she's breathing well."

"And the baby?" he whispered, hardly daring to voice his fear.

Allie smiled. "So far the baby is undisturbed. The little one's heartbeat is normal. But as soon as we get Sophia stabilized, we'll transfer her to the hospital for both their sakes." Since the baby wasn't distressed, Allie opted not to tell him that was one of her main fears. If the time came, she would tell him. But for now, his worrying wouldn't do any of them any good. And maybe the baby wouldn't even reach that point. She prayed not.

"More ice is coming," a man said as he placed two bags of ice next to Allie.

"Get it around her." Allie instructed the women in how to place it.

"Stavros has gone to the next village for more."

"Good," Allie said as she took Sophia's temperature and shook her head. "I'm afraid we may need it. I won't be happy until it's down to 102 degrees. And when it's there, we'll transfer her. Call for an ambulance," she instructed no one in particular. It would take the ambulance at least an hour to get up to Kastro, but Allie knew it wouldn't be safe to transfer Sophia before then, anyway.

"I called," a woman said with fear lacing her voice. "But there are none available. A fire has broken out near Olympia, and all the ambulances are there."

"Okay, we'll transfer her ourselves. Does anyone have a car with air-conditioning?" Allie prayed quickly that someone did. Sophia and her baby would never make it without that modern convenience. Not in this heat.

"The schoolteacher does."

Allie nodded. She didn't even know Stavros had a car. She thought he only had his horse. "Is it big enough to transport Sophia?"

"Plenty big."

"Good," Allie responded.

Later, when Sophia had regained consciousness and her temperature had dropped to 102 degrees, Allie was glad for the comfort of Stavros's Jeep. She didn't know that one could be so luxurious. Stavros was able to turn the rear seat into a bed, so Sophia was as comfortable as she would be if she were in an ambulance. The cool air that blew through the vents was exactly what the woman needed.

Sophia's husband rode with them. He was solicitous in a way Allie wished he had been before, sponging his wife and talking to her, effectively helping to keep the frightened woman calm.

Allie continually monitored the baby. After driving forty-five minutes down the mountain, Allie registered a lowering in the baby's heartbeat. She knew they had just about run out of time. The baby was distressed, and the little one had to be taken from Sophia before it developed problems or even died.

Not wanting Sophia to know how dangerous the situation was for her little baby, she spoke to Stavros in English. "If you can add wings to this vehicle, I would appreciate it. The baby is suffering, and we've got to get to the hospital—stat."

"You've got it," he answered and applied his foot to the accelerator. With lights flashing and horn blasting, he took the curves and turns as fast as any race car driver ever could.

Yiannie looked at Allie in questioning concern.

Allie slightly shook her head and motioned for him to continue to care for his wife. Sophia seemed amazed by the concern her husband was showing and was reveling in it. Allie was glad for the distraction. It was imperative that the woman not become distressed.

As routinely as she had done before, Allie again put the fetal stethoscope against Sophia's tummy. She had to use every ounce of bedside manner not to let her concern show when she registered yet another drop in the baby's heartbeat.

She turned toward the front of the Jeep and spoke in English again. "Stavros, we're going to lose this baby. . . ."

"Five minutes, Allie."

"That's about all the time this baby has. Under normal circumstances, I would perform a C-section myself, but with the heatstroke, I'm afraid for Sophia's life."

"Hold on, Allie. We're almost there." Judging the speed they were traveling, Allie thought Papouli must have been praying for angels to indeed guide their truck. It took less than five minutes for the hospital to come into view. Medical personnel were waiting for them. The doors flew open, and Allie quickly filled in the obstetrician and internist on Sophia's condition while they sped her down the corridor. She watched as Sophia was whisked through double doors and was gone.

Allie knew her job was done.

She had administered medical care that had kept both the baby and Sophia alive, and now she could wait for the men and women at the hospital to do their jobs.

She felt Stavros's arm go around her shoulder and was glad to lean her head against his. "Well done," he murmured.

She looked up at him and smiled. "You, too."

He shrugged his shoulders. "All I did was drive. You saved her life and the baby's."

"That's still not a sure bet," Allie whispered to him, not wanting Yiannie to hear.

"Yatrinna—" Yiannie softly spoke from her side, and Allie reached out her hand for his. "I know my Sophia has only made it this far because of you. Thank you, and forgive me for not supporting you earlier."

Allie smiled a weary but happy smile and squeezed the man's hand. "Kyrios Drakopoulos, all we need to do now is pray that your little baby will be okay. I…" She didn't want to tell him, but she believed that all rational adults had a right to know what she, as their physician, knew. "I'm afraid the baby was distressed during the last part of the drive."

"I know." He looked up at Stavros. "That's why you were speaking in English. But I know you did everything possible. No matter what the outcome, I will always be grateful." Tears formed in his eyes, tears of self-recrimination. "I should have let Sophia come to see you during these last few days. None of this would have happened if I had listened to her and you, rather than to my brother and his wife."

There was no denying that what the man said was true, so Allie didn't insult him by offering empty words. "Because of Stavros's skillful and quick driving"—she looked at him—"I think your baby has a good chance of making it."

Yiannie nodded and walked over to the window. Allie and Stavros left him to his own thoughts and prayers and went over to the chairs that were placed up against the wall. They sat and held hands, a man and a woman in love, giving one another strength. Together they offered prayers for the woman and baby behind the closed double doors.

They didn't have long to wait until they received an answer to their prayers. When the obstetrician walked through the doors, Yiannie turned to him with the look of a man who was waiting to hear whether his world was to be whole again or broken beyond repair.

"You are the father of a healthy little girl." The doctor reached out and shook hands with Yiannie, whose face looked ready to split with joy.

"And my wife?"

"She's doing fine, although the heatstroke is still affecting her. But the internist thinks that by later tonight, she will be nearly back to normal. Holding her little baby was the best medicine in the world for her."

"May I see her?" Yiannie asked.

The doctor nodded. "You may see both of your ladies."

Yiannie started to follow the doctor through the door then stopped. "Yatrinna? Are you coming?"

Allie shook her head. "No. This is your moment. Give her my love and tell her that I'll come back tomorrow to visit."

"Thank you, Yatrinna. For everything," he whispered and went through the door.

"More than just a baby was born this afternoon," Stavros said and nodded after the new father. "I think a man was born, as well."

"Mmm," Allie agreed, and resting her head on Stavros's shoulder, she let him guide her toward the car. She didn't think she had ever been more content.

Chapter 18—Wishes from Her Dreams

On their return trip to Kastro, Allie watched the silvery green countryside slide by her window, with a mature appreciation that had been lacking on her first trip up. They rounded a bend in the road, and Kastro sat gleaming in the sun—like a necklace of rubies and pearls—exactly as it had when she'd first arrived.

She sighed. "It's so lovely."

Stavros turned his eyes momentarily from the road to her. "A land of enchantment?"

She laughed, delighted that he could even suggest it. "As well as a land filled with real people who have very real emotions," she admitted.

"A good place, perhaps, for a hopeful realist to live permanently?" he suggested, and she slanted her eyes toward his.

"A perfect place for a hopeful realist to live permanently," she agreed softly. When a quick smile lit his features, one that held secrets but no verbal answers, she offered up a prayer that his question meant what she hoped. To walk the same path through life that Stavros walked would be the perfect life to Allie.

They pulled up into the village square. As had happened when she'd first arrived, people came out from everywhere to greet the vehicle. Only this time there were more people. And this time they were all smiling.

When Allie alighted from the car, all congratulated her. They welcomed her back and made her feel like the much-wanted member of the community she had yearned to be. She glanced up at Stavros. At that moment, she knew that happiness could have been her middle name.

Understanding, he leaned down and whispered, "Enjoy, my love. I'll be back for you later. I'm going to put the Jeep away." She nodded as the children swept her on a wave of good cheer into the *kafenion*.

Papouli was there, as were all the usual members of the Men's Club. But this time their wives and children were with them, as well as numerous other villagers who had smiled shyly at her during the previous days. There was a festive feeling to the air as everyone cheered Yiannie and Sophia's baby a good long life and Sophia a speedy recovery. Even Tasos Drakopoulos and his wife, Elani, who were sitting together at Tasos's normal table—with a handsome young man whom Allie didn't recognize sitting between them—were raising their glasses in good cheer. In such a small community, the birth of a new citizen was always welcomed grandly. But the extenuating circumstances surrounding this birth made it extra special.

Papouli motioned for Allie to sit next to him at his table. To her surprise, the normally sour-looking Dionysia quickly appeared and served her a cola and *galaktobouriko*—custard pie—along with a smile.

"Sophia's husband, Yiannie, called and told us everything," Papouli spoke for all in the *kafenion*. "We're so proud and thankful for you, Yatrinna." The priest's kind old eyes twinkled their joy in not having underestimated her.

She smiled back at him, her heart warming with love for him as it had for her own father. "I just did my job, Papouli."

As her words pierced the guilt most of the villagers felt over their lack of welcome and support toward her, silence reigned in the room.

Finally, Tasos Drakopoulos cleared his throat and spoke directly to her from his table. "I," he paused and glanced at the young man who sat beside him before continuing. "I apologize, Yatrinna." Allie's brows rose at both his words and his use of her title. "My son"—he motioned to the young man—"as well as the events of the day, have made me realize just how wrongly I mistreated you and the position you represent. I hope you will accept my apology."

"And mine." His wife, Elani, quickly spoke from his side.

Allie looked at the woman. Her Wicked Witch of the West persona had melted away, and all Allie could see now was a woman of remorse who wished only for a second chance.

The young man shifted in his chair, and looking at him, Allie couldn't help but notice that he had the bluest and gentlest eyes she had ever seen. He was also one of the most handsome of men. He would definitely be some woman's idea of a prince. "My parents—" he began, then broke off what he was going to say in order to introduce himself. "I'm sorry, Yatrinna. I'm Dimitri Drakopoulos."

"It's good to meet you." Allie smiled as Dimitri continued, but she had a hard time believing that this very courteous, articulate man was Tasos's son.

"I must take some of the blame for my parents' behavior toward you. I should have been honest with them and told them from the start that I had no desire to practice rural medicine." He shrugged his broad, but unlike his father's, straight shoulders before looking around the café to make sure that he had everyone's attention. "The Angelopoulos family member who has connections with the Department of Health did exert his influence to save this position for me. That's why Kastro was without a doctor for so many months. I declined it without informing my parents that I was the one to do so. I'm very sorry. When Papouli called and told me what was going on—that the ancient and ridiculous feud had been rekindled because of this position—I came directly to set the record straight." He looked back at Allie. "I'm very sorry you suffered because of it."

"Thank you. I appreciate it. And since Sophia and her baby are going to be fine, I more than accept your apologies, and I just ask that this situation—as well as the ridiculous feud—be forgotten. I like Kastro." She looked at Tasos, who now looked nothing like an ogre but, rather, a penitent old man. "Unlike your son, Kyrios Drakopoulos, I *want* to practice rural medicine. And I want to do it as everyone's friend." Her gaze went between that of the mayor and his wife. "Including both of you."

"Thank you, Yatrinna," Tasos rasped out. "I will do whatever I can to ensure that no one ever starts up the feud again."

Even with the apology, a tense silence hovered over the room for a few long seconds with only the sounds of uncomfortable coughing, demitasse coffee cups being returned to their saucers and people clearing their throats heard until the light, lilting voice of a woman—one Allie vaguely recognized—spoke from behind her.

"Goodness," the woman exclaimed and Allie turned and gasped in pleasure when she saw Natalia coming from the direction of the entrance. "As my father has pointed out many times—who even knows how the stupid feud began?"

"Hear, hear," said the villagers, and a sigh of relief seemed to ripple throughout the room.

Allie held out her hand to the young woman after she greeted her father. "Natalia, what a nice surprise. What are you doing here?"

Ignoring Allie's outstretched hand Natalia leaned down and hugged her. "When Dimitri told me that he was driving up here for just one night, I decided to come with him. I missed Baba and Martha," she said simply and truthfully. "I just had to see them and talk to them about some things."

"Eh…Yatrinna, what daughters I have," Papouli exclaimed. His eyes twinkled with a father's love at his youngest child. Natalia smiled fondly back at him before excusing herself when Dimitri motioned that he needed to speak to her.

"That you have, Papouli," Allie said as she watched the exchange between the young doctor and the art student. Allie couldn't help watching them. No one in the café could. They were two of the world's really beautiful people with facial features of perfect proportions and bodies that only fictitious characters should be allowed to have. But as Allie watched, she knew that there was something more between them, or, at least from the expression Dimitri wore, something the man obviously wished was between them.

"Dimitri's going to have to wait a few years if he wants a life with my daughter," Papouli commented sagely. "She's got a very long path to follow before she settles down to family life."

"She's smart. She knows Who to turn to in order to make the correct decisions."

Papouli nodded as they watched Natalia quickly leave the *kafenion* seemingly on some sort of mission. "Yes, I've been very blessed in my children. They all know Jesus as their personal Savior and have the same faith as their ancestors, who received the gospel from the very disciples of Christ."

"Such an amazing lineage," Allie agreed, gazing around the crowd of people searchingly. "But where is Martha? And little

Jeannie Andreas, too?"

"Ahh…" was all Papouli said. But behind his glasses, his eyes danced. "They had something to do. They'll be here soon."

Allie would have asked what they were doing, but a little old lady, who had to have been Papouli's senior by at least ten years, waddled up to her. "Yatrinna, how about doing your job and taking my blood pressure?" she asked, and as all of the people in the *kafenion* seemed to hear her, there were chuckles all around.

In the name of professionalism, Allie refrained from giving a little laugh of her own and only allowed her lips to crack into a smile. "Definitely. I open the clinic at 8:00 a.m. So do come."

"Why can't you take it now?" the old lady demanded, and everyone laughed again.

"You didn't know how good you had it, Yatrinna," said one middle-aged man—a former member of the Men's Club.

"Yeah," another agreed. "You're going to see so much of us, you'll think there are nine thousand of us in this village rather than just nine hundred."

"Oh dear," Allie played along as if the idea made her nervous. "Are so many of you sick?"

"Bah!" the old lady said. "Most of us just want our blood pressure taken."

"But some of us," a man in the rear spoke up, "just want our children looked after."

Allie's smile widened when she saw Petros Petropoulos walk up to her. "Mr. Petropoulos, have you moved back to the village already?"

He nodded his head. "We spent all of last night packing. Just arrived this morning."

There was a gasp of quiet amazement before happy

pandemonium erupted as all the people welcomed Petros back. When they learned Allie's part in his finally returning to his lovely village home, they looked at her with, if possible, even more kindness. Petros and his wife had been stalwart members of the community, and the villagers had not only mourned the passing of his wife and baby, but the loss of Petros and his four other children, as well.

After a moment when the attention was off her, Allie turned to Papouli. They shared a smile. "God really does answer prayers, doesn't He?"

Papouli glanced down at his watch and stood. "Ah... Yatrinna. That He does. But I think the time has come for some more prayers to be answered. Some that have had my special interest for the last several years."

She drew her brows together in question.

"Come." He directed her toward the door of the café. As everybody else seemed to take that as their cue and followed, Allie looked around, perplexed. They all walked out to the plane tree in the village square. It seemed to Allie as if all were waiting expectantly for something to happen.

"Papouli—" Allie started to question what was going on but stopped when the sound of clip-clopping against the cobbled stones of the road could be heard.

She looked in the direction of the sound just in time to see Charger's gorgeous white head round the corner of a stone house. But when she saw Stavros and Jeannie sitting on his back, she gasped. Her eyes widened even more as she took in how the two were dressed.

Jeannie was arrayed like a medieval princess, with a green gown of soft velvet and flowers woven masterfully into her hair, flowers that matched the bouquet in her hands. Stavros was dressed similarly to how he had been the first time Allie had set eyes on him, with a flowing silk shirt and proper riding britches—the prince of her dreams. The castle, highlighted pink in the evening sun behind them, couldn't have made a more perfect background for the fairy-tale scene Allie was sure Stavros had created for her benefit.

The horse halted beside her, and she saw a clarity to Stavros's gaze that had never been there before. It made the hopeful realist in her dare to believe that what she had prayed for—a happily-ever-after with Stavros—might just come to pass.

She didn't say a word.

This was his show.

She watched as he gently lowered Jeannie to the ground. Jeannie turned and walked with all the grace of a medieval princess toward her. Allie wished she hadn't been wearing a tailored suit. She yearned for something flowing and romantic, something to fit in with the mood Stavros had so expertly created.

Just then, Martha, Maria, and Natalia walked up behind her and placed a robe of the softest chiffon over her shoulders. Allie gasped her pleasure as the gossamer fabric wrapped around her like a cloud. She looked up again at Stavros.

He smiled, and just as teachers at school performances were experts at doing, he motioned for Jeannie to commence her part in this lovely, romantic show.

"Yatrinna—"

Stavros cleared his throat.

Jeannie smiled and started again. "I mean, Princess Allie." She indicated the bouquet in her hands. "These flowers are for you from my father, who awaits your permission to take you on his white stallion, Charger, up to the castle."

Allie reached for the flowers, and while bringing the

arrangement close to her nose and inhaling the fresh, sweet fragrance, she lifted her gaze toward the prince and spoke. "I would be honored to ride up to the castle with your father—Princess Jeannie."

Jeannie's face split with a smile. "That's what you're supposed to feel like, Yatrinna. A princess! Isn't it wonderful?" A good-natured laugh went around the crowd at the girl's exuberance.

Leaning down, Allie kissed the little girl's cheek and said in agreement, "It *is* wonderful, Jeannie." She turned her gaze up to the girl's father again. "Wonderful," she said to him and continued with, "it makes me feel as if I am part of a fairy tale."

His eyes crinkled at their corners, and as he reached down and pulled her up behind him, he whispered, "Darling Allie, it is a fairy tale. But the best kind. One that has God in the story. He is the One who leads this hero and heroine."

"Oh, Stavros," she whispered into his ear. "Not even I could have imagined that such joy was possible to feel."

He chuckled softly. "That, from my fairy tale–loving lady, is a great compliment." Then, more softly, for her ears only, he spoke words that he had needed to say for a long time. "I'm so sorry, Allie, for all that I ever said to you. You *can* have it all. Your profession—which saves lives—and the happily-ever-after." The first cool breeze anybody had felt since the heat wave started nearly a month ago blew across the cobbled streets just as he finished. All murmured at how wonderful it felt against their skin. Stavros laughed and held up his hand to the wonder of it. "You can even have cool air, my love."

"I'll gladly take it all, Stavros," she said, and as she wrapped her arms around him, she marveled at how so much had changed in her life in such a short period of time. Her gaze met that of Papouli's, her "fairy godfather." The older man shrugged and motioned toward the cross that sat atop the church. His gaze very clearly said, "With God all things are possible."

Nodding and smiling in agreement, Allie mouthed the words *thank you.* She knew then what the dear man's prayers of the last several years had been—that Stavros would not only find his faith once again but the love of a woman, too. The fact that a man she hadn't known had been praying for her to come into the life of the one she now hugged close was nothing less than one of those amazing things of God. *Thank You, God!*

After Maria, Natalia, and Jeannie fixed her robe so that it draped perfectly over the horse's flank, Stavros clicked his cheek and directed Charger to walk at a slow pace out of the village. The village children—young and old alike—ran alongside and cheered.

Allie leaned forward and asked in his ear, "Why are they cheering?"

He chuckled, a laugh that she felt rather than heard. "Maybe because there are a whole lot more people around who like fairy tales—nice ones—than I ever realized." And feeling her questioning gaze, he turned his head halfway to her and said, "In a moment, darling Allie, I'll answer—and ask—everything. For now, just enjoy the ride."

She did. A ride of enchantment, a ride of wonder, but mostly it was a ride of love. The path the stallion took up to the castle was different from the one they had walked together. It meandered along the backside through silvery olive groves filled with cicadas that serenaded their upward journey and the cool breeze that pleased their skin. The green-and-golden valley shimmered below them, and the sky above was the ethereal Greek blue that poets and bards had written about since the

220

beginning of the written word. As they followed the path farther and farther up, Allie knew that she and the man whose back she hugged close to her were exactly where God wanted them to be. She squeezed her eyes shut and silently gave thanks for the miracle of knowing.

When they came to the entrance of the castle, Stavros swung himself off the horse, then reaching up for her, his hands lightly grasped her waist as he lowered her to the earth. He didn't let go of her but gently pulled her into his arms. "Darling Allie," he spoke against the top of her head. "I have one very important question to ask you"—he took a deep breath and, stepping back half a pace so he could look directly into her eyes, he sighed out—"but I'm going to do it right this time and ask a few other ones first."

She nodded. She was quite certain of the one important question. She wondered about the others.

His shirt sleeves billowed out in the breeze as he continued. "I know your feelings about God, but do you feel confident we believe in a way that would be compatible to joining our lives?" he asked with a solemn quality to his voice that she respected and appreciated.

Her eyes searched his. What she saw there—a man with a deep faith in Christ—made her confident of her answer. "Since you have reaffirmed your belief, dear Stavros, yes, I do believe that our walk with God is compatible."

He lightly ran his fingers down her cheek and smiled, one of love and friendship before he softly continued. "Darling Allie, how would you feel…about becoming Jeannie's mother?"

Tears—liquid joy—touched Allie's eyes at the question. She knew how much he loved his daughter. For him to ask this of her was the highest compliment he could pay her. She reached up and touched his forehead. "Dear, dear Stavros, I would be honored to be Jeannie's mother. Her legal mother," she qualified. "I would want to adopt her so that should we be blessed and able to have children together, she would be certain that it would never make her any less my daughter."

Tears now washed his eyes, and they fluttered closed. "Thank you, Allie." He sighed before opening his gaze—his very vulnerable gaze—to hers again.

"For what?"

"For wanting children with me. For wanting to be Jeannie's mother. Her natural mother didn't even—"

She placed one finger against his lips, stilling his words. Shaking her head, she said, "Don't judge her, Stavros. We don't know what went on in her mind, but I'm sure it couldn't have been anything pleasant. Just be thankful she left you with that wonderful little girl." Allie smiled. "I know that I am."

"Oh, Allie—" He hugged her close and rubbed his hands over her back. "What did I do to deserve you?" he questioned into the wind. "You are so wise, so beautiful, so—"

She stilled him with her mighty laugh and took a step back from him. "What I am is impatient. Are you going to ask me *the* question, Stavros, or shall I ask you?"

He let loose with a generous laugh of his own. "Wouldn't that ruin the fairy tale if the princess asked the prince for his hand in marriage?"

She slowly shook her head from side to side. "Darling Stavros, I don't think anything can ruin this fairy tale. . . ."

As her words were swept out over the land on the cool, north wind, he lowered himself to one knee. "Allie—Princess Allie—I love you. Would you do me the honor of becoming my wife and of giving to me all your ever afters?"

With her robe fluttering out and around her, Allie reached down and pulled him to stand tall and straight before her. Looking up at him, she replied, "Dear Stavros, I would be honored to become your wife, the mother of your daughter, Jeannie, and the mother of any other children whom God might grant us. My ever afters are your ever afters from now and for always."

He shook his head at the import of her words. "I love you, Allie," he murmured, just before his lips captured hers, and Allie's words of love remained unspoken, but not unsaid, as her lips told him what was in her heart. She loved him, loved him more than she had ever imagined she could love someone.

And someday soon they would marry, and she knew that because their union was ordained by God, they would live...

Happily-ever-after...

Key to Mood Boards

Top right to left; bottom right to left

Frontispiece: woman with double French braid (Allie) / rundown clinic / Greek mountain village / white horse and rider (Charger & Stavros)

Chapter 1: old bus / mountain road / top of a castle / angry chicken

Chapter 2: village in summer / tortoise / donkey / rundown clinic

Chapter 3: plane tree branches / village house / *kafenion* (café) / Psalm 37

Chapter 4: interior of village apartment / village road / woman sleeping / village house

Chapter 5: lovely bathroom / girl helping (Jeannie) / veranda / flip-flop

Chapter 6: Byzantine church building / Greek coffee / blue door (priest's house) / figs in basket

Chapter 7: happy family / bath towels / door handle / spending time with horse (Charger)

Chapter 8: beautiful valley / cleaning supplies / EKG machine / Greek village road

Chapter 9: market / fresh oregano / homemade rose-petal jam / pregnant lady (Sophie)

Chapter 10: medical emblem (caduceus) / *frappé* (iced coffee) / times long ago / salt &pepper (two sides of a feud)

Chapter 11: painting supplies / woman painting wall / pails for hauling bath water / well-earned soak in a tub

Chapter 12: broken window / fairy-tale book / Holy Bible /

romantic day-dream

Chapter 13: woman remembering being kissed / man fixing cut electrical wire / purposeful walk through the village / *kafenion* interior

Chapter 14: rosebushes trimmed / exhausted pregnant woman / waiting room ready / dreaming of dinner

Chapter 15: view from castle / romantic picnic / happy couple / golden Mediterranean valley

Chapter 16: trip through forest / woodsman's hut / sad children / love is in the air

Chapter 17: heat of the day / heatstroke / people praying / mad-dash to the hospital

Chapter 18: fairy-tale princess girl (Jeannie) / dreamy castle / romantic ride / wedding dreams

Review

I hope you enjoyed reading this book that is loosely based on my year in a Greek mountain village. If you did would you please let me know? Leave an Amazon Review (that would help my rankings on Amazon a great deal) or send me a direct note…or both! I'd very much like to hear from you.

There are several books in this series, From Greece with Love, *so you will meet the characters again.*

Next… in *From Greece with Love,* Natalia's story is told in:

New York Welcome

*Why did Natalia return to Kastro for the night? What does Natalia
need to talk to her father and sister about?
Hint: She's met someone who is about to change her life —
She's moving to a city filled with castles of another kind:
New York City!*

Available now!

Set in New York City at Christmas time

(Inspirational Romance with Mood Boards)

Next… in *From Greece with Love,* Martha's story is told in:

Love Comes Unexpectedly

What news does Martha have?
Hint: She's about to move away from her home of 56 years to open a
gift shop in the land of her mother's ancestors:
Ancient Olympia, Greece!
At her age, she isn't expecting anything other than enjoying being the
proprietress of a gift shop, definitely not love. But American widower,
Leo Jones, has other ideas…

Available now!

Set in the home of the ancient—and modern—Olympic Games
during the lovely days of summer

(Inspirational Romance with Mood Boards)

Do you want to read about the *real* St. Nicholas as described in Chapter Four of *New York Welcome*?

St. Nicholas & Christmas:
The Teenager Who Gave Us the Celebration

When the Early Church was still one, St. Nicholas lived. Treat yourself to an eye-opening and fun journey (taken with a modern teenager) into the early life and times of young St. Nick; the boy, then man who was to become known as Santa Claus. Although almost forgotten, we don't have to look far into his long life (AD 250-345) to see the real reason he is so closely associated with Christmas. Teen Nicholas was indeed a gift-giver. But the biggest gift he gave was the CELEBRATION of Christmas itself!

Available now!

Drawing

Join my MAILING LIST to get updates on this series, my other books, etc. and…become eligible to take part in the drawing that will be held July 1, 2023 for an 8″ reproduction of an ancient Greek amphora urn similar to the one below.

MelanieAnnAuthor@gmail.com (type "Mailing List" in the subject line)
Instagram: @melanie_ann_author
Facebook:facebook.com/MelanieAnnAuthorPublisher

Printed in Great Britain
by Amazon

13857684R00137